The Heroin Heiress

GRANT BUTLER

THOUGHT CATALOG Books

THOUGHTCATALOG.COM
NEW YORK • LOS ANGELES

THOUGHT
CATALOG
Books

Published by Thought Catalog Books, an imprint of the digital magazine Thought Catalog, which is owned and operated by The Thought & Expression Company LLC, an independent media organization based in Brooklyn, New York and Los Angeles, California. For bulk purchasing inquiries, please visit shopcatalog.com/about.

This book was produced by Thought Catalog. Cover by KJ Parish.
Visit us on the web at thoughtcatalog.com and shopcatalog.com.

Made in the USA.

ISBN 978-1-949759-38-9

For Marc

1

My uncle once told me, "Show me the most attractive person you can think of and I'll show you someone who is sick of their bullshit." I didn't know it at the time, but that is the best advice anyone has ever given me.

I broke up with my girlfriend Allison about 2 months ago. I really cared about her, but I found out she was cheating on me with some guy. I'm not gonna lie, it hurt pretty bad. But that was quickly replaced by rage. The kind of rage that ceases to be an emotion, but rather becomes a living, breathing entity. It didn't help that she immediately broke down and tried to play the victim. Especially when I found out the dude had been hooking her up with drugs.

It was beyond insulting. She had zero right to play the whole injured party card. Sorry sweetie, not gonna work. When she realized that, she tried to get angry and started yelling, calling me every name in the book.

"Who are you to judge me?" she kept screaming, over and over.

At this point, I think her attitude was more appalling than the actual cheating. It was like watching a child throwing a tantrum in the middle of the mall. Allison even managed to do the same stomping up and down. I had to admit, I found it funny. But eventually I just turned around, walked out of her apartment, and didn't look back. As I was driving away, I saw her run out of the apartment and try to race down the sidewalk towards my car.

I kept on driving, not sparing her a glance. Right on cue, the non-stop calls and texts started coming later that night. You all know the ones I mean.

First, there are the ones that are frantically apologizing and begging for your forgiveness. Then there are texts or emails that try to act all nonchalant and ask about your day and life, as if nothing had ever happened.

Then come the spite-filled ones that try to act all tough and insult everything about you. If you are a guy, there is almost guaranteed to be a shot at your masculinity or prowess in the bedroom. For the ladies, a low blow at your appearance with a passing reference to some other girl they've had their eye on will be the weapon of choice. A bit of gaslighting usually comes about here. The offending phrase is usually something like "Why are you being so mean to me?" or "You are being very immature."

Any sort of message like this usually ends with something like "Fine! If you are gonna be like that I don't need you anyways. (Insert rebound's name here) is so much hotter anyways."

But my personal favorite is when they send you a late-night text, usually between one and three AM that goes along the lines of "I really miss you." The kind that is designed to tug at your heart just enough to get your attention and lure you into talking, but nothing that requires an actual apology. I can't even tell you how many times Allison messaged or called me before I blocked her.

It was almost like seeing a mental patient off their meds. Of all the girls I have broken up with over the years, Allison put in more effort to contact me than all the others combined. It was kind of stunning. She was a huge fan of alternating between I miss you and I will burn your house down depending on the moment.

Needless to say, I didn't answer or respond to anything Allison said. I didn't block her immediately because it was hilarious watching her go to pieces after SHE cheated on me. But like most sane people, I got tired of it and blocked her number, email, all that good stuff.

I went on with my life and everything was good. Or as good as things could be.

Starting last month, I started getting these weird emails. At first, they just contained simple stuff. The email address was one I didn't recognize. One of those obvious throwaways.

"Hey."

"How are you?"

Then came the weirdest of all. "Do you have a girlfriend?" I thought it was just spam, so I marked it as such and didn't give it a second thought. Then, the text messages started coming about a month later.

"Good morning, Vince."

"How is work going?"

"What did you have for lunch?"

I was confused about who was messaging me, not to mention a bit suspicious, so I didn't answer. But a couple days later, on the first day of March, my phone dinged to indicate the same number had messaged me again.

"Do you miss her?" There was a picture attached, along with a smiling emoticon. Just guess who it was?

Allison. Same long blond hair, green eyes, and wide smile. How not shocking at all. She made that email account to message me and got a new phone for the same reason. I had put all of this behind me and here she was, trying to worm her way back into my life again? Unbelievable. The girl had major issues. At that moment, the searing rage returned and I messaged back.

"You cheated on me and now can't leave me alone? Bye. Don't you dare try to contact me again or you will be sorry."

I blocked the number, tossed my phone aside, and thought that would be the end of it.

Coming home from an errand about a week later, I was driving when I got a phone call. It was my neighbor, Mrs. Arlington. Sweet lady. We lived in a new duplex and I really felt comfortable there. She treated me like a son and I won't lie, she was like another mom to me. I would help her with anything she needed around the house and occasionally she would cook for me. Best apple pie you've ever had. Not to mention she was very supportive when I broke up with Allison.

"Hey Mrs. Arlington, what's up?"

"Vince, are you at home?" She sounded concerned.

"No, why do you ask?"

"Because I keep hearing noises from your place. Sounds like someone is inside. I swear I can hear laughter. A woman's laughter."

My entire body went numb at this. "I'm calling the police. Don't worry about doing anything unless someone tries to break into your place."

"Ok my boy," she sounded simultaneously relieved and tense.

As soon as I hung up with Mrs. Arlington, I called the cops and told them someone broke into my house and my neighbor heard it. I gave them the address and they said they would be there immediately. Then, I called Mrs. Arlington back and told her the cops were coming and to watch the door to my place. Very slowly, I continued driving to my duplex. I stayed on the phone with her until the police arrived, which didn't take too long.

The officers kept watch until I arrived. I have to say, there is nothing quite like coming home to the sight of the police waiting for you. As I approached, I had to remind myself that it really was my house they were parked in front of. Mrs. Arlington was standing there on her front porch, all concerned, her long red hair flapping in the wind. I have never been more grateful to have her as a neighbor. Neither she nor the cops saw anyone try to leave. The police informed me they searched the place and found nothing had been broken or destroyed. Now it was my turn to look around. When I did, it appeared nothing had been stolen.

That bothered me more than anything. To know someone had been there for seemingly no purpose. No valuables taken, nothing trashed, just....a silent presence. A laughing presence apparently. Usually being home made me feel content. Peaceful. Now it just made me feel tense. I made sure to thank Mrs. Arlington for keeping an eye out and everything. Just as the cops were about to leave, one of them spoke up.

"Is that yours?" Officer Mansfield asked, his jowly face contorted into an expression I couldn't quite read.

"Is what mine?" I had no idea what he was talking about.

"That," he said, pointing outside the sliding door onto the back porch.

There, positioned right outside the porch, was some sort of rag doll. I wasn't sure what it was at first, but then I saw it looked a bit like me. It had the same blond hair and brown eyes. The clothes looked like something I've worn many times before, khakis pants and a polo shirt. The doll looked like it had seen better days. Then I realized it looked like it had been repeatedly stabbed or cut, because the stuffing was coming out of the body in several places. My legs felt like rubber at that moment, but that wasn't the worst part.

The doll was hanging from the tree right next to our building, hanging by what looked like the end of a noose. A very well made and realistic one. We all went outside and sure enough, the doll of me was hanging from a noose. It slowly swung back and forth in the wind, like some sort of sick wind chime.

"I.....don't really know if it's mine," was all I could get out. "I guess it is now." Mrs. Arlington patted me on the arm consolingly.

"You can stay with me tonight Vince," I immediately accepted.

"That's very kind of you ma'am. There isn't much we can do about this, but be sure to keep an eye on things and we will do the same. If you need anything, call us and we'll be here ASAP," Officer Mansfield informed me.

"Thank you, I will."

With that, they left. I gave Mrs. Arlington a big hug and got my clothes and stuff. As I packed my bag, I couldn't help but feel like they were somehow tainted. I couldn't get out of there quick enough. I immediately went into Mrs. Arlington's house and crashed on her couch, because that seemed like the only thing to do right now.

2

Although Mrs. Arlington lived right next door and we both occupied the same crisp white colonial style building, her house now seemed like an entire world away. Her house had what people liked to call "character." It all felt so lived-in, the kind of place you might pass a pleasant afternoon with a favorite aunt who never thinks you have enough food on your plate. When you walk inside, you can't help but expect a friendly dog to greet you enthusiastically as you cross the threshold.

Her kitchen is one of the first rooms you pass. The refrigerator is covered with so many magnets and trinkets from her various trips, you can barely see the color of the actual refrigerator. Everywhere you look there is a city; Tampa, Richmond, Boston, Cabo San Lucas, it's all there. For most people, it seems that fridge magnets and bumper stickers have replaced luggage stamps as the telltale sign you traveled somewhere. My living room is filled with books of various places I've been; first editions and autographed biographies. I find the sight of all those worn leather books on the shelves quite calming.

After I put my stuff away in the guest room and settled in, I amused myself for a bit by watching some bad television on Netflix. Mrs. Arlington was kind enough to leave me alone for the evening, only giving me a quick heads up to let me know she made some cheesy potato casserole for dinner. I felt like I had no appetite, but once I started eating, I didn't stop until the plate was clean. Eventually, I faded off into a restless sleep. I woke up to a faint cluster of sunlight cascading through the windows. Checking my phone, it was 9:27 am. I lazily rolled out of bed and fed myself some cereal before my best friend John came over. After the usual pleasantries of asking how I was, we just sat around the living room with the TV on for background noise.

"Come on," I spoke up suddenly after about an hour. "We're going out."

"Where?" John asked.

"The movies,"

"You sure you want to do that?" It wasn't a rhetorical question, he just wanted to make sure I really wanted to go to a movie.

"You bet your ass I do. I didn't let Allison control me when I was with her. I didn't let her cheating control me, and I sure as hell am not gonna let her bullshit control me now. I am not gonna hide from little miss gone off the deep end. That's what she wants me to do. Keep me all stored away to play with me whenever she wishes, that's what this was all about. She wouldn't hurt me. This was the same girl who once had a nervous breakdown over almost hitting a possum with her car. No, what she wants is to see me all holed up inside and having a meltdown because of her. I wouldn't let the fact that she screwed some random guy get to me, so she just took it up a notch. All in the quest to try to make sure that my world still revolves around her." Without noticing it, I had raised my voice steadily when speaking to John. But just saying all that out loud made me feel better.

"Good point."

"Yeah. Besides, I've seen this shit a million times. If someone really wanted to kill you, they wouldn't beat around the bush. Talking about crime is like talking about sex, the ones who talk big never do it. So what movie shall we see?"

"I'll let you pick man." That was John for you. Always a considerate guy.

†

It appeared that I was in luck this morning. While there were no new movies out I wanted to see, the big multiplex about half an hour away from here was having one of those special events where they screen old classics on the big screen. Even better was the movie being shown; *Dirty Harry*. The movie was set to begin at 12:30 so we left Mrs. Arlington's about 15 minutes later. As I was driving away, I couldn't help but cast a glance at my part of the building. I don't know what I expected, a fleeting shadow making its way across the windows perhaps. But everything was still.

Driving through town on the way to neighboring Glenbury, it all felt so surreal. The cops had told me that in addition to being on the lookout for Allison and keeping watch on the house, they were also informing security at work about how they should treat her as a risk. I had no desire whatsoever to discuss this situation with anyone at work, so I was glad the police were treating it as a sensitive matter.

I've been living here in Greenbriar, Illinois for about 5 years since I started working at Greenbriar University. My official title is Associate professor of Anthropology and History. The town of Greenbriar itself is a decent place and the university is a cool place to work. It's a good-sized college, not so big that classes are unmanageable, but big enough so that the locals are always complaining about noise or something. I don't know why they bother opening their mouths, everyone around here knows the college is the biggest employer and revenue earner in the area. The local restaurants and stores would shrivel up and die without student bucks, so believe me, the city goes out of its way to "reasonably accommodate" us. Greenbriar is a respectable, middle-class town but if you go about 15 minutes west you'll find this seedy gas station that marks the beginning of Parkfield. About a year ago, there was a massive drug bust in a trailer park there. Can't say it surprised me at all. I strongly suspect the guy Allison hooked up with is from Parkfield.

Deep down, I wasn't worried. Because if Allison had really wanted to hurt me, she would have done it already. The girl had no patience or long-term planning ability. It was also worth noting that she was also the world's biggest bullshitter. Know what the difference between a bullshitter and a liar is? The liar believes their own nonsense, whereas the bullshitter knows they're full of it. Ever since I met Allison at that coffee shop I could tell she was a lot of bluster and whatnot.

✝

Ah, the movies. No matter how old I get, there is nothing like going to a movie theatre. Pulling up to the big 20-screen multiplex made me feel automatically better. Once you enter the dark theater and the movie starts, you can't help but begin to feel like you've entered another world entirely. Which is the entire purpose of a movie theater. It's why it pisses me off when I see people texting during a movie. I paid good money to be entertained by something on a screen, and that screen is not the one where some Tinder user swiped right on you.

Like any decent movie goer, John and I had stocked up on snacks before we set foot in the place. He is a Skittles man, whereas I am a fan of peanut butter M&Ms. As we parked the car and walked inside, I could feel them jiggling around inside my pocket. The morning was a dreary grey, with a brisk wind and a faint sprinkle of rain dotting the sidewalk. Typical March weather for around here.

As we were buying the tickets, I immediately got a whiff of the greasy, buttery smell of movie theater popcorn. The smell got stronger as we passed the ticket booth and the concessions stand on our way towards theater number 5. Since the theater was mostly empty, we had the pick of virtually any seats we wanted. We settled on two aisle ones on the upper left-hand side. Sitting there in the theater as the previews began, I felt myself beginning to put aside anything going on outside. But just before the movie started, I did have one realization that made me put it all into perspective. This was nothing new; not at all. Because long before Allison was addicted to drugs, she was addicted to attention. She was used to it. As a beautiful young woman who ran a bar, she could count on it. When we were together I was happy to give her plenty of attention, which made her happy. For a little while.

Everyone always says the same thing, "They didn't always used to be like that." Of course not, because if they had, you would be beyond stupid and borderline insane for not avoiding them like the plague. In most relationships, regardless of whether they are good or bad, the beginning is usually quite different from the middle or end of it. Hell, most of us didn't used to be the way we are either. People grow, it's only a question of in what direction. But no, Allison didn't always behave like this. At least not to me. I can't speak for anyone else.

Here's when things started to go south. Allison would piss and moan about not seeing each other enough or not doing enough things together. But when I made the effort to see her or tried to accommodate her, all she would do was stare at her phone, pretend I wasn't there, or offer me only nonchalant attention. It was like she was a kid that had finally gotten the new toy she had been begging for incessantly, but when she finally got it she no longer cared.

After this began happening, she also started getting suspicious of my work. She would ask questions about my students and various appointments I had throughout the day. When I mentioned a female student's name, you could see her eyes narrow and practically hear the paranoid thoughts swirling through her head. At first all she did was tease me about it. "Oh, are you sure that's what she really wants you to tutor her in?" or "She sits in the front huh? Can't say I blame her for that. At least she has good tastes."

But then she started being just downright unpleasant about it. Which in hindsight makes sense. They always say that in relationships, the worst cheaters are also the people who are most nervous about getting cheated on. Because if you are a serial cheater, the idea of someone being unfaithful in a relationship is a very real concept to you. Somehow, I can't help but wonder if part of the reason Allison wanted to get inside my house was to see if I was there with another girl. Sadly, that wouldn't surprise me at all. In fact, I'm amazed she didn't randomly come see me at my office when I was at work for that exact same reason.

I had nothing to worry about. Allison wouldn't seriously hurt me. This was just a really fucked up way to get attention. Unfortunately, this time she had gone a little too far. She was about to get her wish, but she wouldn't be getting the kind of attention she was hoping for.

†

After the movie, we went back to Mrs. Arlington's place. Stepping foot back inside, I was more grateful than ever she let me stay here. It was truly a home filled with memories; warm, happy experiences. If I had to stay in some hotel, it would feel like I was in the witness protection program. Not to mention I wouldn't have been able to sleep at all. While I have never stayed in a hotel for quite this reason, it's hard enough to sleep in a hotel under the best of circumstances, much less when you are hiding out at one. Since Mrs. Arlington didn't have a ton of food and I didn't dare touch anything in my house food-wise, that meant I had to make a run to the grocery store. When I got to the supermarket located in the heart of Greenbriar, I saw that it was moderately crowded. About what you'd expect on a Sunday evening.

Grabbing my cart, I wheeled it in-between aisles as I tossed in some stuff; cereal, spinach, Italian salad dressing, brown and serve dinner rolls, a fresh loaf of ciabatta bread, and a bag of Idaho potatoes. Homemade meatloaf sounded good to me, so I picked up some ground turkey and beef along with the spices I needed. The last thing I wanted to get was a frozen pizza. I walked towards the end of the store where the frozen section was and pulled a pizza out of the freezer, the chilly air blasting me as I reached inside. As I was digging through the boxes, I looked to my left and saw the reflection of someone in the freezer door. Normally I would have just brushed it off and went on with my day, but this time I felt myself focus on the reflection. As I did, I felt like I had been standing in the freezer for three hours.

Blond hair, same height, and dressed in something trendy Allison would wear. Since she had her back turned to me, I couldn't immediately see her face. My hands tightened over the cart's handle as I frantically reassured myself that it wasn't her. It was just too crazy. But then I remembered that too crazy seemed to sum up the situation perfectly. As I was arguing with myself, the blond turned around to grab a tub of ice cream.

False alarm. I felt my breathing start to relax and I made a beeline for the checkout. Fortunately, the lines had thinned out by now and I found myself at the front in no time. As the middle-aged guy rang me out, I could still feel the adrenaline rushing. What would I have said to her? Hopefully I would never have to answer that question. That's why they call a breakup a breakup. Once it happens, piecing a relationship back together is impossible. Even when couples do manage to get back together after a breakup, they don't have the same relationship they did before.

†

As I drove home, I was relieved that work was tomorrow. Nothing beats that for getting your mind off personal issues. But deep down, something told me that I would see Allison one last time. I just had no idea when.

3

I woke up early the next morning and got to work right on time. It was another dreary morning, but instead of a light sprinkle outside there was a consistent shower. It wasn't bad when I left Mrs. Arlington's, but by the time I parked the car it was really coming down. The few remaining patches of snow lingering in the parking lot had been hardened into piles of grey and black sludge. Grabbing my black umbrella, I hastily made my way indoors. We had a department meeting this morning at 10 am, which I always found quite dull. But this time, it was over something far more important than trivial matters like who was getting the retired professor's old office.

No, this was a state mandated lecture on addressing opiate abuse. As I got to the meeting room on the second floor, I noticed there was an open white box containing donuts and other pastries placed in the middle of the conference table. I could tell just by looking they were stale. The rest of my colleagues were scattered around the room, chatting nonchalantly.

"Alright gang," the department chair Dr. Flanigan called out as the signal that it was time to begin. We all gathered chairs around the table as he readied the power point he had prepared for the meeting. "As you all well are aware of, heroin abuse has reached a fever pitch all around the state, and not just with students. They want us to keep an eye out for all members of our university community; students, staff, and faculty alike."

The dull lecture droned on for what seemed like forever. Flanigan made sure to include all the usual clichés about keeping your eyes open, good communication, and being part of a community. He kept scratching his ginger beard as he lectured on in his gravelly voice that was far better suited for describing British colonial history than heroin abuse. While this subject was indeed important and Flanigan meant well, the lecture wasn't groundbreaking or anything.

As soon as his talk was over, I headed back to my office. Getting back into the routine felt good. Ascending the steps to the third floor, I was soon back in the history department with its winter green walls, dark wood trim, and maroon carpet covering the floors. The department was quiet with the scent of instant coffee lingering in the air. At the front of the department was the desk of the department secretary Noelle, a woman in her mid-40's who was currently playing some game on her phone. She barely glanced up as I brushed past her without making a sound. Past Noelle's desk, the department conference room was on the right next to the kitchenette and the faculty offices were all on the left, mine being five doors down from the front.

Unlocking the door, it felt good being back in my office. It was untainted by any unwanted visitors and their psycho toys. Nothing here but mounds of papers, books, and my superb view of the massive pine trees decorating the courtyard, the envy of everyone else in the department. Right next to my computer was the framed photo of me with my parents at their beach house in Florida. That was when Mom had her grey hair cut short and Dad had just started coloring his hair. My parents had retired and moved down there a few years after I got my position here. I'm very happy for them and visit them every summer; they always say they don't miss the winters up here one bit.

Leaning back in my chair, I took a deep breath and relaxed. In this context, everything that happened over the last few days seemed unreal. Like it didn't even exist outside these walls. It was a nice consolation prize that I didn't get engaged to Allison or something before I found out how screwed up she was.

All my friends who are married or in a committed relationship look at me funny. Here I am, in my early 30's and not married, engaged, or anything of the sort. Their favorite line is something like, «You are a great catch; nice looking, good job, intelligent, plenty of fascinating interests. Tons of women would love a guy like you." But when pressed to name said women, they can't seem to think of any. What they're really asking is, "What the hell is wrong with you that makes no one want to date you?" The odd thing is, my older married colleagues are all super understanding of it. Sometimes when I mention I am not married, I get the look. That pleading look that screams, "Get out while you still can."

On the other hand, people love to give me a wink and joke that the only reason I took this job was so that I could be around college girls for the rest of my life. Usually the person who says this quickly adds that they envy me. Perhaps they are onto something. I know plenty of colleagues who have picked up a student here or there. Personally, I can't blame them. Plenty of sexy young women coming to class knowing that you can help them, it's almost unfair. Believe me, plenty have showed up asking for extra credit or for their last exam to be graded on a curve, just like in some awful porno. I'll admit that I've thought about it, but I wouldn't dare go near that. Too much opportunity for trouble.

Since it's college, it's not illegal or anything for faculty to be involved with students per say, it's just "frowned upon." But it's a very risky situation if something goes wrong. For example, imagine if my unhinged former girlfriend also happened to be my former student. That would make the situation ten times worse. The potential for trouble aside, the general idea still doesn't sit well with me. You wouldn't be able to shake the idea that a college girl was just with you because of what you could do for her. Additionally, the gossip that a professor was dating his former student would get out quickly and you'd be a pariah at faculty events. Believe me, stuff like that spreads like wildfire.

†

Logging off my computer, I stood up and stretched before I grabbed my coffee cup and locked the door behind me. It was about time for me to head to my scheduled lecture that took place at noon. After topping off my coffee in the department kitchenette, I was on my way. The 10-minute walk to the classroom went by quickly and before I knew it, I was face to face with my students. I made some small talk with them until it was time to begin. This week began the section on the Civil War. Brushing some lint off the sleeve of my black sweater, I straightened up and began to talk.

"What is history? That depends on your perspective really. One person's history is another person's reality. At some point, you will read about events that my generation, myself included, lived through. The way we view it now is often completely different than the way people viewed it at the time. Let me give you an example. Here we are in Illinois, the birthplace of the Lincoln mystique. Take a short drive and you can visit his tomb. Odds are good that most of you drive cars with Land of Lincoln on your license plate. He is on our money, our landmarks, and in our national consciousness. But while he was alive, Abraham Lincoln was barely elected President in 1860 and not unreasonably thought he would be defeated for reelection in 1864. He was generally unpopular throughout his presidency, had harsh critics of all political persuasions, and the South began seceding from the Union before he even took office. Literally half the country absolutely loathed him and yet despite all this, he became the man who held the Union together, abolished slavery, and become known as the most revered American of his time."

I paused while I allowed this statement to sink in.

"So, what changed? His life and presidency were the same, weren't they? That didn't change, but the way people perceived it did. Subsequent events occurred that caused people to reevaluate their opinion of him. Some of that took place while he was still alive. But his death transformed him from a man into an icon. The nature of death often forces people to evaluate or reevaluate the individual who has died. In Lincoln's case, he was publicly shot on April 14, 1865, which also happened to be Good Friday. In an era of deep religious sentiment, that symbolism alone was quite powerful. Add in hindsight from the messy era of Reconstruction that followed, people couldn't help but wonder, what if? Even after all this time, people are still asking that same question."

I waited a moment before continuing. "Let's go one step further. All odds were against Lincoln becoming President. He had no formal education, little political experience, and no national name recognition. Mary Todd Lincoln came from a slaveholding family and some of the President's in-laws fought for the Confederacy during the Civil War. When running for President in 1860, Lincoln was up against men who were all more well-known and theoretically more qualified than he was. And yet, he ended up outshining them, and in the eyes of history, he permanently stands above them all."

I paused again to take a sip of my coffee. "The Civil War itself was a curious event; the result of a perfect series of events where Lincoln's election happened to be one of the last chips to fall into place. For the most part, people back then had no idea that events of their daily lives were slowly leading them on a collision course towards violence, chaos, and bloodshed. They never imagined that seemingly isolated incidents, like a new state being admitted to the Union, would create events that would eventually lead to four years of war. A war in which hundreds of thousands died and countless others were wounded. Their treatment? Primitive medicines which included opium, known to us as an offshoot of heroin." This caused a few students to look at me more intently than before.

"Taken separately, events from many years prior seemed irrelevant to the present situation. But it wasn't. What happened before directly played a role in the present. As we shall see, events came together perfectly, causing a crisis of unprecedented proportions. History is far more than memorizing simple facts; it seeks to explore why the world as we know it exists as it does. My hope is that by giving you the best tools I am able to, it will help you think critically about the past in order to understand both the past and present."

I went on for the rest of the lecture without any problems and left work later that afternoon. As I was pulling out of the parking lot, I couldn't help but remember something. They say Lincoln predicted his own death because he saw part of it in a dream. While I certainly didn't experience anything like that, I knew I would be seeing Allison very soon.

4

Since it's Mrs. Arlington's habit to go out of town every year around this time to visit her brother in Tennessee, I've been crashing at her place alone for a bit. She told me on Monday that she would be leaving Friday, which happens to be today. When I got home, she was just pulling out of the driveway in her grey Chevy. She saw me and gave me a honk and a wave. I hope that wherever she's going, the weather is nicer than it is here. While it may not be raining today, the wind is absolutely brutal.

Because I could use some company, I called John and invited him to swing by later this evening. He used to be a bouncer at a club in Chicago and now works as a personal trainer, which was how we met. I used to work out at a gym he used to manage. While John looks like someone you wouldn't want to mess with, being 6'4 and 300 pounds of muscle, he's actually the most approachable guy ever. But believe me, he can handle himself in a tough situation. He also knows plenty of, shall we say, *interesting* people. After the incident at my house, his cousin Eric helped us set up a security system to monitor my building. When there is any movement occurring, either outside or within my part of the building, it automatically sends a notice to both John's phone and mine. From there, we can watch a live stream of any camera. John also called a few contacts of his to sweep my part of the duplex for anything suspicious. As expected, they didn't find anything.

After Mrs. Arlington left I started going through my mail. Most of it was the usual ads and junk mail. One piece of it was a plain white envelope addressed to me, the only thing inside was a single piece of paper.

"Next time the version of you at the end of a rope won't be a doll. See you soon."

I didn't recognize the writing. It was a real mess to read, a bunch of scribbles all jumbled together. Come to think of it, I don't think I have ever seen Allison's handwriting. I immediately checked the camera to see if it picked up anything, but nope. Just the regular mail delivery guy. I also called the cops to follow up with them on what I had just received. They came by and took the note.

Later, John came by with some takeout he had picked up on the way. While we dug into the Caesar salads and cheesy bread he ordered, I told him about my little delivery.

"Dude, I'm so sorry," he eventually said over a forkful of lettuce.

"Appreciate it man, but don't worry. I'm cool."

"Yeah? How are you staying cool?"

"It's like the old saying goes. You have nothing to fear but fear itself. Allison doesn't want to actually kill me or anything, she just wants to scare me and intrude on my life. For starters, if someone wanted to seriously kill me, they would just go ahead and do it. Why would you repeatedly warn someone you wanted to kill?"

"That is so true," John nodded in agreement, his black hair bobbing slightly in the air.

"But it's deeper than that. When she was inside my house, she didn't burn the place down or wreck the place. Hell, she didn't even go through anything. Does that sound like someone who really wants to hurt you?"

"Good point man."

"Believe me, I'm wary and cautious for sure. But not afraid."

We had finished eating and were watching some bad reality TV when my phone buzzed. It was a notification from the security system.

Immediately, I grabbed my phone and opened the live streaming function. The camera that had its senses tripped was the one located outside my part of the house's front door. Moving quickly, I got up and went back to the guest room where I grabbed the pistol I had brought with me in case of emergencies. Although John had helped me get it and practice with it, I never had to use it before. I hoped this time would be no different.

It had quieted down since I had been out, so I could clearly see what was going on outside. In my haste I had said nothing and had momentarily forgotten about John, who had noticed my reaction and was standing up, instantly alert. I held up my phone and said the two words I had been expecting to say for days; "She's here."

Allison. Just standing there in front of the door. From the looks of it, I wasn't sure she had the slightest idea of where she was. Allison looked like she was either sleepwalking or higher than a kite. It was the eyes that gave it all away: unfocused, dilated, and just flat out weird looking. I won't lie, it was an unnerving sight. It also didn't help that I barely recognized her. Her hair was a greasy mess, her clothes made it look like she had crash-landed in the jungle or something, and her previously beautiful olive skin looked almost grey. It was bizarre, but that wasn't the worst part.

At first, it looked like she was stroking a cat or something. Then I realized what it was. A teddy bear. An ordinary child's teddy bear. Apart from it being a bit worn and dirty, it was no different than the one you might get at the store. Weird.

Then, I noticed something else. Not only was she stroking it like a pet, I realized that her lips were moving.

No. There was no way. It couldn't be. Was she actually talking to it? Well, that was easy enough to figure out. The cameras were equipped with audio so all I had to do was use the function and listen for myself. After taking a deep breath, I switched on the sound.

I didn't recognize the voice when I first heard it. Allison always had the most beautiful voice; the kind that lured you in and made you want to listen all day. This person, it was like listening to Allison pretending to be a kid again.

"Hey there Mr. Bear, what should I do? You wanted me to come here, told me so yourself. But what now? I left the doll just like you said. You told me if I was good you would give me something special." She kept walking around in circles, like she was waiting for something.

I thought the doll of me she left was disturbing enough, but this was some next level freak show. It was like she had totally lost it. At this point, I was just hoping she was stoned out of her mind, because if she was sober......let's just say that wasn't a good sign.

"You've been so good to me, you understood me when other people were mean to me, when HE was so mean. So what do you want me to do?" She then lifted the thing up and held it to her ear, like some kind of insane sea shell she was expecting to make a sound.

"Hey man, the police are on their way," John suddenly said. I thought I heard him say something when I was watching the cameras. Good man.

I've known the guy for years and he used to work as a bouncer, so I know he doesn't scare easy. But when I looked up, the look on his face was something I will never forget. I nodded my head to show I heard him. But he too quickly resumed watching whatever it was Allison was doing. The whole thing didn't seem real. She then moved so suddenly we both flinched. Now she was looking down at the bear with a wide smile, as if she had just experienced some great epiphany.

"Thank you so much for helping me get rid of that mean guy, the one who came between me and Vince. When he sees how sorry I was and how I made things right everything will be just as it was. We will all be one big happy family! And I owe it all to you!" She swept the thing up in her arms and gave it a big hug.

I couldn't watch it anymore. She had officially gone insane. I didn't even want to think about 'that mean guy' she got rid of. Fortunately, this was right about the time I heard sirens approaching. I suddenly realized that my right hand, the one that was holding my gun, had begun to sweat. John continued watching the whole thing on his phone. All I could do was stand there. There was no way I would be going outside while she was there.

Eventually I heard a car door slam and a slight commotion out front. From what we saw, they subdued Allison and took her away gently, but firmly. Flanked by an officer on both sides and one in front to open the door, they put her in the back of one of their squad cars. I'm not exactly sure where they plan on taking her, but they could put her on the Moon for all I care.

Then they came and spoke to me and Johnny. We showed them the footage of her outside my house and stuff. They were extremely grateful and asked us to email their department a copy of the live stream we had watched. After this, they told us another unit had searched Allison's apartment and had documented what they found. Apparently, she had managed to get into more trouble besides stalking me. Because of this, she was heading for a psychological evaluation. Then the officer in charge asked me a final question.

"Do you know if she was seeing anyone after you?"

Wait, what? You are seriously asking me who she dated after we broke up? Did you not just see her outside my apartment talking to a toy??

"No, all I know is she was cheating on me with some guy."

"Thank you," but now it was my turn to ask a question.

"Why do you ask?"

The officer didn't say anything, but he turned to the woman next to him who handed him a folder. He gave it to me without a word. Opening it, I could tell it was Allison's apartment. Or what had once been Allison's apartment. It was a complete wreck. You couldn't tell what furniture had been where, or what the layout of the place was. It looked like a tornado had ripped through everything in sight. But that didn't really bother me. The paper all over the walls though, that was a different story. It looked like every inch of wall in every room, including the bathroom, was plastered with paper.

But that paper wasn't blank, not by a long shot. There was writing covering virtually every free inch of paper. The writing was in various colors and had been written using crayons, pens, and sharpies. The paper itself was equally varied; yellow and blue sticky notes dotting the walls along with pages ripped from notebooks and legal pads. The handwriting itself varied in style and size; massive untidy cursive dotted Allison's living room while tiny, neatly written letters decorated the space on her bedroom wall. Some of the pictures had been zoomed in, allowing me to make out what was written on them. I realized it was the same phrase written over and over again.

"I should've never messed with him. He won't leave me alone. Someone please help me."

It felt like someone had just dumped a bucket of ice down my back; now the officer's question made sense. After I handed back the folder without saying a word, one of the other officers spoke up

"Don't worry man, she'll be going to a mental hospital for a while. I've seen things like this a million times. People can get a bit obsessive. But I gotta say, that stuffed thing is creepy as hell."

"What makes you say that?" I couldn't help but ask, even though I totally agreed.

"You know that feeling you get when you are a kid and there is that one toy or something that you can almost feel watching you, no matter what you do?" I nodded. "It's like that. But don't you worry, we made sure that thing went with her. She won't be able to bother you again."

After that, the remaining cops drove off and we went back inside Mrs. Arlington's house. I felt relief wash over me as I shut the door behind us. That was it, the visit I had been waiting for. Although I must admit, I wasn't expecting anything like that. Without saying a word, John turned the TV back on and we went back to watching some trashy reality show. While I usually hate watching any reality TV, it suddenly felt nice being able to watch the nonsense from someone else's life for a change.

5

After Allison was carted off, I did my best to get things back to normal. But believe me, it wasn't easy. I mean come on, seeing your exgirlfriend carted off by the cops to the loony bin is quite a sight. The day after the cops took her out of my hair, I called Mrs. Arlington.

"Hey Mrs. Arlington."

"Vince! So glad to hear from you. Is everything ok?" Concern broke into her tone. She was under no illusion about what was possible in this day and age.

"Yeah everything is fine. They just took Allison to a mental institution."

"That's wonderful. My God, that sounds so horrible to say." That was your typical Mrs. Arlington, or Sharon as her close friends called her. No matter how many times she insisted I call her by her first name, I always addressed her as Mrs. Arlington. Out of respect you know?

"No, I get you, believe me. They can do something about her there. I just wanted to let you know what was going on here, so you could make plans accordingly."

"Thank you Vince, always so thoughtful. But if you don't need me for anything, I'm planning to stay here a bit longer."

She's letting me stay in her place with my friend because of my psycho ex-girlfriend and she thinks I'm the thoughtful one? Mrs. Arlington could move to the shadiest neighborhood in existence and I would gladly follow her, just to have her as my neighbor. They just don't make neighbors like that much anymore.

"Not at all, take your time. Be safe and have fun!"

"Same to you my boy, double. Thanks for calling Vince!"

"Always, take care."

I wasn't sure quite what to do now. What was I supposed to do? How was I supposed to feel? There is nothing quite like seeing someone you used to date carted off by the cops. I was relieved, but I also couldn't help but enjoy it. I usually don't enjoy seeing someone thrown into a mental hospital, but usually said person didn't screw some other guy behind my back.

After a little while, I did what any of us do when we are curious about anything; I went to the internet. Once I parked myself in front of my laptop, I began looking up how to cope with a relationship gone wrong. While I never thought it would be possible, some of the stuff I found actually put my situation to shame. But that's the rule of the game anymore; think you have it good or bad, there is always a bigger fish out there. I can honestly say that none of my previous relationships has ever ended on a note even faintly resembling this one, so the whole situation is a bit of a learning curve for me.

A lot of the advice I found when I typed in 'what to do when your ex-girlfriend goes insane,' was stuff I was already doing; change the locks, alert your neighbor, all that good stuff. But other comments were helpful because they were just downright hilarious.

"Went insane? What the hell's the difference from before?" had earned a lot of upvotes.

"If she left you she was obviously off her rocker," was another gem.

Weirdly enough, perspective had made this all darkly funny. It wasn't like Allison had broken in and left some sort of animal sacrifice on my bed. So long as I didn't find a dead cat left on my front porch as an offering one day, I really didn't have much to worry about. That's the beauty of the restraining order I was in the process of getting.

The other part of me couldn't help but wonder if the crew of *Impractical Jokers* or something was gonna pop out to say it was all a stunt. I knew it wasn't, but it all seemed so surreal.

Slowly, things began to feel alright again. I got into a routine and it didn't change. One of the first things I did when I moved back into my own home was to have all my bedsheets changed and the comforter washed; nothing like crisp new sheets to make you feel better. Most other things in a house are extras, but there are three things you absolutely must have: a comfortable place to sleep in peace, a bathroom, and a kitchen.

I was looking over my shoulder less and sleep was coming easier to me. Eventually, Mrs. Arlington came back from her trip and things began to go back to how they were pre-Allison. We still had the camera system installed, but why get rid of it? It could come in handy sometime. Plus, we also tended to forget it was there.

The last traces of winter began to fade away and spring was upon us. St Patrick's Day was surprisingly warm and since it happened to be on a Saturday this year, John and a couple other friends of mine had a blast at Finnegan's, a local Irish pub about 20 minutes away from town. I had a few shots of rum, my typical go to shot; John, on the other hand, was totally drunk. But a good time was had by all.

About three weeks after Allison was taken away, it was late one night when I suddenly woke up from a deep sleep. Looking around my dark room, I could feel that I had broken out in a cold sweat and was still feeling the effects of a bad dream.

In the dream, I was sitting on my couch reading a book when out of nowhere, someone began shrieking at the top of their lungs. Shrieking is different than yelling or screaming; it's more animalistic. This was immediately followed by a sharp rap at my door and I sat frozen on the couch as someone was insistently knocking for me to answer it. Then the knocking suddenly stopped and I heard something else; something, or someone was laughing. It started quietly at first, but steadily grew until it seemed to be everywhere. Not just any laughing; it was that unfriendly, cold laugh people use when they know something you don't and plan to use it against you.

That was when I woke up. My eyes slowly began adapting to the darkness as I frantically looked around my room. I immediately grabbed my phone; the time said it was 3:12 AM. Checking the cameras for any sign of trouble, I saw no sign of any disturbances outside. I got up, turned on the lights, and checked all the locks and everything; nothing out of place there either. I peered through the blinds covering every window; just a quiet evening outside.

In my head, I knew everything was as it should be. The dream itself was already beginning to slowly trickle away, like ice melting in the palm of your hand. I don't usually dream, and when I do, I usually forget them right away. To help get back to sleep, I got myself a drink of water. For good measure, I had a little snack of a few pretzels as well. Food is always way more helpful at getting back to sleep than some sleeping pill that just turns you into a zombie. Just think of every Thanksgiving dinner you've ever been to. After gorging yourself, there is nothing else to do but crash on the couch and nap.

I remember that every Thanksgiving dinner when I was a kid, my grandma used to make this pumpkin pie. To this day, I have no idea what she put in it, but it was delicious. But about an hour after eating it, you felt like crashing on the couch and not getting up until Christmas. Almost all my relatives have tried to imitate the recipe, but no one can get it quite right. It's like trying to make a Wendy's Frosty or something in your kitchen; it's just not the same.

As I got back into bed, I turned the TV on and put the volume on low for some background noise. After channel surfing through some old cartoons, I left it on TV Land before falling back to sleep.

I woke up a few hours later, the sound of rain lightly pounding on the windows. For a moment, I forgot where I was. But then I realized the TV was on and I remembered waking up from a dream in the middle of the night. Weirdly enough, I felt like I had gotten a great night's sleep. For some reason, spring rain always puts me in a good mood and, since it was Saturday, I decided to make myself a real breakfast. No hastily eaten granola bar or instant oatmeal today. No, today was french toast day. Personally, I have always preferred french toast or waffles to pancakes.

Firing up the stove, I got down to business. There are two ways to make french toast; with legit french brioche bread, or not at all. Trust me, once you make french toast with this bread, you will never be able to enjoy it any other way. It is also fantastic for a grilled cheese. The sweet, thick bread is just like a sponge, so it works perfectly.

As I continued cooking, the buttery smell steadily filled the air, making my house seem the most welcoming and content it had been in a long time. When everything was ready, I grabbed the sticky bottle of maple syrup out of the fridge and it was time to dig in. I don't know if it was because it had been so long since I had made it, or because I was starving, but it tasted fantastic. It wasn't long before all that was left was an empty plate with a tiny puddle of syrup on it. I had just finished eating and was sipping some orange juice when my phone rang. I studied it for a moment before answering it.

"Hello?"

"Hi, is this Vince O'Malley?" a professional sounding man asked.

"Depends on who wants to know." I wasn't about to immediately give any personal info away after all that had happened.

"Of course. This is Dr. Edwin Burton. I am the current chief of staff at the Longford hospital where one Allison Dunbar was being treated." Great, just what I wanted to hear.

"Well isn't that just swell," I spat out harsher than I intended to. "Look Doctor, just tell me whatever it is you have to say and leave me alone. She's caused me far more trouble than she's worth." I felt bad for a moment because it wasn't the guy's fault, but at this point I couldn't be bothered to care.

"Certainly, and I apologize for having to call you. It's simply that the police mandated we inform you if there was any news in her case. Forgive me, but I am not quite sure how to tell you this."

"Just go ahead and say it," I sighed with a deep breath.

"I'm sorry to have to tell you this, but Allison is dead. She was found dead in her room three days ago." That definitely was not what I was expecting him to say. In that moment, I felt nothing; my entire body felt numb, my mind equally subdued. I felt like everything was on autopilot.

"How?" That was all I could think of saying.

"When she was first brought here, I could tell right away she might be a problem case. She was always too quiet. Whenever another patient or staff member had a problem with her, she never reacted or lashed out. Those are the ones you need to watch out for. But it was her drawings that concerned me the most."

"Drawings?"

"Oh yes," he paused, drawing out the last syllable. "When she was brought here, that was the only thing she would do; draw pictures. But those pictures were definitely not the healthy things one wants someone to draw."

"Oh I can imagine what you mean,"

"I know you can Mr. O'Malley." I was beginning to feel better about this guy. "She would draw endless pictures of what looked like people getting stabbed. Most of them looked like families being murdered in their beds. Soon, her entire room was filled with them. This was one of the most concerning signs we witnessed. The other one we observed was that the only time she would voluntarily speak was when she spoke to the stuffed animal that was brought along with her."

"Mr. Bear." How could I forget?

"Correct. Approximately four nights ago, Allison had been particularly difficult. She began fighting with both fellow patients in the common room, as well as with the staff assigned to her. This was a new development, as she had never been violent or even remotely aggressive before then. After the staff subdued her, she began screaming. At one point, she even started screaming in what we believe was Russian."

"Wait, what?" Allison could barely speak English, let alone a foreign language. Her texts were always riddled with typos and I swear, she couldn't go a few sentences without saying the word 'like'.

"Yes, one of our orderlies is originally from Ukraine. She helped us translate Allison's ravings to mean 'blood will be spilt' or something like that."

"That's insane, and I know that's ironic considering who I am talking to," I said as I ran my finger absentmindedly across the rim of the glass containing my orange juice.

"Believe me, calling this matter insane is quite an accurate statement," he agreed before continuing. "Because a patient screaming will severely agitate other patients, she was appropriately sedated and put back in her room. When the staff went in the next morning to check on Allison, they discovered that she was dead. The autopsy revealed that the cause of death was suicide by means of ingesting pills. The initial autopsy revealed it was a lethal cocktail of sleeping pills and painkillers."

"How could she get them? Did she steal them from the doctors or something?"

"Believe me Vince, we keep a VERY strict watch on our pill stocks, with every pill being accounted for. She was also completely searched for anything on her arrival, metal detector and everything. But we never thought she would think to hide pills in advance inside the teddy bear. She was brought immediately to the hospital after she was taken in by the police. We even searched the bear itself by feeling around for anything suspicious. All that security found was what appeared to be the inside stuffing. That was the most unbelievable part, she didn't even smuggle in whole pills. She had crushed them up beforehand so they were ready. Nothing inside the bear came up as flammable or anything, so we had no reason to look any further."

"I don't blame you doctor, it is unbelievable. How could she have known to smuggle crushed up pills inside a stuffed animal before coming over to me?"

"Without a doubt, this truly is the weirdest case of my career, and that is really saying something. But, now you know. You don't have to worry about her any longer."

"Thank you for telling me. Oh and sorry for being rude earlier."

"No problem, I know what happened in your situation. I wouldn't ever want to hear about some psycho ex again either."

"One last question," I asked as a sudden thought came to my head.

"Of course."

"Do you think she had any inside help or anything?" I heard a deep sigh on the other end of the line and when Dr. Burton spoke again, his voice had dropped to a hush.

"I would love to be able to flat out deny it, but believe me, at this point I'm not ruling anything out. I'm having some people I absolutely trust look into the matter here. I take great pride in professionalism, but believe me, I know the potential for abuse at mental hospitals. But at this point, I have no reason to suspect anything."

"Good plan, and thank you for keeping me in the loop, Doctor. You take care now."

"You take good care of yourself as well, Vince."

With that, the call was over. Allison was over. Even now, I have no idea what to think or feel. There isn't exactly a roadmap for this sort of thing. I won't lie, it's a major relief that I won't have to worry about her anymore. There is just one thing that bothers me. How was it possible she was speaking Russian?

6

After I got the news about Allison, the first few days that followed were a bit weird. It all felt so unreal, like it couldn't possibly be happening. Part of me was expecting to get some phone call saying that it had all been a mistake. But that never came. After about two weeks, it finally began to sink in.

She was really gone.

I wasn't sure what, exactly, I should be doing or thinking. I was glad she wouldn't threaten me or anyone I cared about, but I definitely didn't want it to come to this. It all seemed so....unsatisfying. I don't blame myself or anything, because everything was entirely her decision. I couldn't understand her mindset if I tried, and believe me, I tried. I learned a long time ago, if someone truly has their heart set on something, there is nothing you can do.

All the same, I decided to see what my fellow internet users had to say about the matter. Now, if I thought it had some amazing things to say about your ex going insane, that was nothing compared to what I found for "what to do when your ex-girlfriend dies?"

"Bust out a bottle of champagne and turn on 'Ding Dong the Witch is Dead' from *The Wizard of Oz*." That one honestly made me laugh harder than I had in a long time.

Another poster chimed in with "If my ex ever died I would drive a stake through her heart to make sure she didn't come back."

There were a lot of other amusing comments combined with sincere advice about what to do, along with links for information about coping with grief. Oddly enough, it was all quite helpful in processing what happened.

I eventually decided to do the same thing any sensible person does when they experience something mentally and emotionally trying; stock up on ice cream and watch a lot of TV. There is just something inherently soothing about ice cream. It can instantly make a bad day better.

But this occasion definitely called for binge watching my favorite shows while stuffing my face with Vermont's finest ice cream. So off I went to the store to stock up. As I locked my front door, I turned around and was greeted by a cool, but still pleasantly sunny day.

†

As soon as I arrived in the ice cream section, I grabbed two pints of Ben and Jerry's; Chubby Hubby and Mint Chocolate Cookie. But since they were having a sale on Breyer's, I decided to get some of that too. How could you go wrong with Cookies and Cream? Before I knew it, I was actually enjoying myself; buying all this junk food made me feel like a kid again. The dude ringing me up didn't even say a word. Honestly, people don't even need an excuse to gorge themselves on ice cream anymore.

Once I got home, it was time to get down to business. Pint of ice cream in one hand, I pressed play on my laptop and turned on *The Walking Dead*, a show I was so behind on it wasn't even funny. Oddly enough, Allison hated it. Said something about it being too violent and creepy. I know, ironic right? I, on the other hand, am a man of simple pleasures. I appreciate zombies and ice cream; combine the two and that is something special indeed.

While the episodes began streaming, I felt myself relaxing. This was the most at ease I had felt in a long time. With a tub of ice cream in one hand, spoon in the other, my feet up on the coffee table, and the survival efforts of Rick Grimes and his crew unfolding before me, the whole Allison thing seemed to fade into the background. Mint Chocolate Cookie was always my favorite flavor, so I started with that one. Its refreshing taste was delicious as always. For the first time in a few months, I was feeling like my old self. It was like I'd been in a deep sleep and had finally woken up after a nasty nightmare. You look over your shoulder for so long, you forget to live any other way. I was gonna make sure I had a lot more moments like this.

The next few hours seemed to melt away. Before I knew it, it was 11 p.m. Logging out of Netflix, I began browsing the web after I checked my email. The usual clickbait stuff was entertaining enough. Not to mention the always amusing cat videos that never fail to make you smile. Scrolling down, something else had caught my eye.

"Local man found dead in house fire." I clicked on the article and began to read it.

Daniel Millstone, 43, was found dead in his home late yesterday morning. Emergency responders were called by Millstone's neighbors, who could smell smoke coming from the Millstone residence. Upon arriving on the scene, Fire Chief Jim Bradley confirmed that a small fire caused by a cigarette not properly extinguished was the cause.

The article went on to quote Chief Bradley as saying, "Mr. Millstone appeared to have fallen asleep while smoking and the cigarette butt was not properly extinguished at the time. We believe that started the fire and Mr. Millstone died from smoke inhalation. Fortunately, his family was out of the house at the time of the incident. They were able to inform us that Mr. Millstone worked third shift as a medic at the Longford Mental Institution and often came home tired and smoked to unwind."

Wait a minute. That was the same place Allison was.

Immediately, I felt my body tense up. I tried to make myself relax, telling, myself they didn't say smoking kills for nothing. People died from falling asleep while smoking all the time. The article went on with the usual obituary stuff; date and location of birth, parents, family, you know the drill.

But towards the end there was one other thing that caught my attention.

"He had a natural affinity for languages and spoke at least four fluently; French, Chinese, Italian, and Russian."

Russian? Isn't that what Allison was screaming in before she died? That was a little odd. But I read on, telling myself that it was just a coincidence. The obituary went on to list a few of the guy's favorite things. His favorite movie was the Daniel Day Lewis movie *There Will Be Blood*.

I was almost done reading when I saw that. Initially, the only thing that came to mind was that the guy had good tastes in movies. Pausing over it, I began to think. In the hospital, Allison had screamed, "blood will be spilt." At first, it had just seemed like some random outburst. But what if something had gotten switched in translation? I knew from experience that the titles of books or movies were notorious for that. There will be blood, blood will be spilt? Is it just me, or is that too much of a coincidence? Especially since Dr. Burton had told me himself that he couldn't rule anything out yet. As I reached the bottom of the obituary, I glanced over one of the final sentences.

"Despite working third shift, he always made it a priority to have breakfast with his family when he got home from work, no matter what." Third shift; also known rather appropriately in this case as the graveyard shift. The same shift that Allison most likely died during. But this was all hypothetical of course. No reason to suspect anything.

Just as I was about to click out of the article, I saw there was a picture to go with the obituary. It was of the Millstone family. According to the caption, it was the most recent one they all took together. Nice family by all appearances. They looked like the type of family that would be perfectly at home in some advertisement for a new SUV. But what caught my attention most of all was of the daughter. Average looking girl. But it was what she was holding that caught my attention.

It was a teddy bear. But not just any old teddy bear.

Mr. Bear.

I knew it was him because it had the exact same worn look that I had seen on my phone that night. Shit. Just seeing that thing again pissed me off. I immediately closed the link and shut my laptop. I immediately told myself it was nothing.

So what if he gave his daughter a teddy bear? Happens all the time. Yard sales, hand me downs, what's the difference?

I didn't know what exactly to think at this point. Maybe I am just being paranoid. After everything that's happened it would be the most natural thing in the world. Either way, Allison was dead and no fucking teddy bear would ever change that.

7

A few days after I saw the Millstone obituary, I went down to see my parents in Florida for Easter, and it was a fantastic visit. I don't think I have ever needed a vacation as badly as that one. Not only did we have our usual feast of turkey, ham, mashed potatoes, beet salad, and an assortment of pastries, but I also spent plenty of time relaxing on the beach and swimming in the ocean. I came home on the Tuesday following Easter and got back into my usual routine. The days alternated between brisk sunshine and dense rain, but I didn't mind. I've always found spring rain to be rather soothing. Everything in my world was back to normal. Maybe, just maybe, it was all behind me.

Or that's what I thought. It had been about two weeks since I returned from Florida and classes would be done for the summer soon. I had just finished grading some essays and to celebrate, I felt like treating myself to something good for dinner. I decided to order some pizza with breadsticks and was immediately glad I did. It was delicious as usual. There is nothing like the feeling of eating takeout pizza while sitting on the couch and watching a movie. I was in the middle of scarfing down my meat lover's pizza when there was a knock at the door. Since I had nothing to worry about anymore, I got up without hesitation. Although you can bet I checked the camera outside first on my way to the door. Old habits die hard. When I looked through the peephole, I saw this woman I had never met before.

"Who is it?" I asked.

"Hi Vince, you don't know me." Way to state the obvious, sweetie. "But I know who you are. I'm Chloe, I was an old friend of Allison's when we were kids."

Great, just great. At this point I wasn't afraid or anything, there was just rage. What the hell could she possibly want from me? Here I was, minding my own business, and she has the nerve to interrupt me? I stood there for a moment, rooted to the spot. There was no way I was gonna let this girl in my house. Not without a VERY good reason.

"What do you want?" I could see her flinch through the camera feed at my tone, but I didn't care. Hey, she could have given me some notice that she was coming. That way I could have pretended like no one was home.

"I know you are upset about Allison, but I swear to you, this is important." I couldn't tell you how long I stood in the hallway, but eventually I heard myself say the words.

"What is it?"

"I knew Allison years ago, I have information about her past."

"Meet me tomorrow at Brewster's Coffee shop. It's about 30 minutes from here." I still wasn't keen on letting her inside.

"I know where it is." Chloe didn't dare say another word. Perhaps she was worried if she argued or spoke too much, it would make me change my mind. Maybe she was right.

"3 o'clock, and don't be late." She still didn't say anything, but she nodded in comprehension and walked off my porch. I took a deep breath.

At this point, I had no idea what to expect. But I might as well get this over with. I went back to my couch and tried to return to my pizza. But somehow, my appetite was significantly diminished. Oh well, plenty for tomorrow. Leftover pizza is one of the great joys of life. When I went to bed that night, all I could do was thrash around and stare up at the ceiling. After a faint bit of sleep, I rolled myself out of bed and got ready to leave.

†

Brewster's was a cozy little coffee shop located at the heart of Greenbriar. Its dark burgundy walls and overstuffed leather sofas make you feel automatically relaxed the minute you walk inside. Baristas there know your name, your order, all that good stuff. I walked in and there was Chloe, perched on one of the overstuffed brown leather armchairs. Seeing me, she instantly sat upright. Her long black hair was tied back in a ponytail and she stuffed her phone in the pocket of her black jeans as I walked in.

"Give me a moment," I said as I pointed to the counter. She nodded in understanding. If I was gonna take a trip back to Allisonland, I was gonna need my fix. As I approached the counter, I saw that Evan, my usual barista, was working today.

"Making your usual right now Vince," he called out smoothly. Good man, no one made a double shot caramel latte like Evan did. As I handed him the money for my order, he waved it away. "She already paid for it. Said to make your usual and it was on her," he added as he pointed to Chloe.

"Thanks Evan, you're the best here." I said gratefully as I turned back to her. That was a surprisingly nice gesture. Hopefully it wasn't preparation for more bad news.

"Thanks for the coffee." I sat down across from her as I took a sip.

"No problem, it's the least I can do. A stranger showing up at your front door with more Allison drama after so long. You have no idea who I am, and yet here I am, wanting some of your time to talk about something I couldn't blame you for not wanting to talk about for the rest of your life. But I promise you, it's something you deserve to know, and as soon as I'm done, I will be gone."

Her words came out like she couldn't say them fast enough. Chloe then took a deep breath and looked down at her hands, the universal sign for 'I don't know how to say this.' I glanced at her hands too; fingers laced together and clasped tightly on her lap. Poor girl was way more on edge than I was. Looking at how nervous she was made me relax a bit. It also didn't hurt that she wasn't bad to look at.

"It's ok, go ahead and say what you came to tell me. I won't interrupt you. I guess it'll be good to get some answers for once. " I spoke up in what

I hoped was a nonthreatening, inviting tone. Since she looked up at me and seemed to relax, I guess I did something right.

"Ok. Allison and I were neighbors growing up. I first moved to the neighborhood she lived in when I was about 7, and I lived there until I was about 20. I will never forget the first day I met Allison. We had lived there for about a week when her family came by to introduce themselves. She and her parents were nice, but for some reason I felt on edge around them. I didn't know what it meant at that age, but I knew that I didn't feel comfortable around them. As a kid, you have no idea how to understand and process emotions and observations. It wasn't that they weren't nice, but there was something more to them. Something that you couldn't really name, but you could sense. My parents invited Allison and her parents to our house once for dinner and it went fine. But my parents never went out of their way to socialize with her parents and Allison and I only saw each other sporadically. Our families were cordial, but not close. The funny thing is, they could have been the ideal neighbors. Respectful, courteous, but they definitely kept to themselves."

She paused to take a sip of the bottle of water she had in her purse, a shiny black leather thing that looked like it cost an obscene fortune.

"About nine years after we moved there, I was in the living room one night doing my homework. I was sitting on the couch when I heard a noise, so I looked out the window. There was her father, Mr. Dunbar, who had just gotten home. At first, I didn't think anything of it. But then I saw who he was with; some woman who was most definitely not Mrs. Dunbar. Allison and her mother had gone out of town to visit Allison's grandmother, while her father had stayed behind. From what people have told me since, I think Allison's grandmother didn't like Mr. Dunbar. At first, I had no idea what was going on. He looked super tense and the woman looked all nervous too. But when I saw them quickly go inside and the light in the master bedroom went on, I could figure out for myself what happened. The rest of the night, I had no idea what to do. But I ended up telling my parents exactly what I saw. They thanked me for being honest with them and told me not to say a word to anyone."

When she said that, I couldn't help but wonder. Did Allison know something was up in her parents' marriage? But Chloe had more to say.

"Allison and I weren't in the same classes, so we didn't really see much of each other. She and her mother came back from their trip a week later and as far as I could tell, they had no idea what happened. They all carried on as normal. Or as close to normal as they could get, because I truly wonder if they ever were 'normal' if there is such a thing. I think when there is a big family secret, every member of the family reacts to it, even if they have no idea what exactly it is they are reacting to. Not unlike how I felt about Allison's family, they can sense it even if they can't understand it. Her parents began to argue more than they had in the past. I could see them in the windows; my room on the second floor had an excellent view of the kitchen windows where I could watch without them seeing me. All parents argue at some point, but this was different. I will never forget their expressions; pure masks of bitterness and resentment. Sometimes they would blast music to try to cover up the noise if Allison happened to be home. After that, things got worse. It became an open secret in town that things were bad at their house. You were afraid to see or talk to Allison or her parents because you didn't want to say the wrong thing. Everyone could feel that something had gone sour with them. About 3 months after I saw that scene while doing my homework, Mr. Dunbar left home one night and didn't come back."

"You're kidding me?"

"Wish I was," she shook her head sadly. "Nope, it was in July, an incredibly humid Friday. I heard his car leave the garage about 7 that night and it never came back. He was reported missing, so everyone went out looking for him, but no one found anything. He never came back, and to this day, no one knows what happened to him. I also never saw the woman he brought to their house again. But I know that she worked as a legal secretary for one of the town's big shot lawyers. Beautiful young woman, too." Part of me couldn't believe what I was hearing, but the other part was taking it in and wasn't the least bit surprised.

"Allison never said a word about this. She told me her parents divorced when she was young and she occasionally saw both of them." Chloe nodded faintly in understanding.

"That doesn't surprise me. I don't think she ever truly came to terms with what happened. Especially with Mrs. Dunbar's behavior after her father vanished. Usually when your husband disappears, you are a wreck, a total basket case. But not Allison's mother. I never really spent time with either of Allison's parents, but I would much rather have spent time with her father than her mother. You ever have the sense that someone is putting on an act that is always on? That was Mrs. Dunbar. She was always perfectly dressed, makeup always on, but she was a very reserved person. But once Allison's father disappeared, it was like this fresh, vibrant, exuberant woman came out. Believe me, people began to talk. You can imagine what they said. Word also began to get out about Allison at school. I had a few friends who were in classes with her. She began acting out, getting into fights, the usual type of misbehaving. They never liked her much to begin with, but after Mr. Dunbar was gone, dislike turned to fear. Fortunately, I didn't bump into Allison too much after that. She and her mother moved out of town about a year later. I haven't seen them since." I sipped the last of my coffee before I asked the question that had been on my mind since last night.

"Wow. I have to ask, though, how did you find me?" She looked like an unbearable burden had just been lifted from her shoulders. Chloe was now the most relaxed I had seen her.

"I always wondered what happened to her. We all did. Allison was a beautiful girl, always was. Even if you didn't know her, she had this way of making you root for her. My mom was online for something or other about a month ago and she stumbled upon the news that Allison had died. Someone had shared the news on Facebook. It said in the obituary where she used to work, so I went there, where they told me what she had gotten into, which was how I got your first name and where you worked. So naturally, I looked it up on the college website and then went to the address book and now here I am." That made sense, but she had one last thing to say. "I know she put you through a lot, and I truly feel for you. I won't insult you by asking you to take pity on her or anything, but I just thought I should tell you what I know."

"Thank you for that, and for the coffee."

"Thanks for listening. I am sorry to have brought her back up, but I honestly didn't know what else to do."

"It's ok. It was the truth. We should never apologize for being real. Since you've been so kind to come find me, I guess I should tell you what I know." I took a deep breath before telling her my side of things. I hesitated at first, but the story came out easier as I spoke. I had never really confided in anyone for months about this, and it felt oddly helpful to tell the story to a complete stranger who could relate. Chloe flinched a few times during the story. She even shed a tear when I told her about Allison being taken to the hospital, but she never once interrupted me. When I finished, we sat there in silence.

"I am so sorry," is all she could say. I didn't say a word, but I nodded. She stood up from her chair and stretched. "Thanks again for your time, Vince. You are a good man. She didn't deserve you, but you did your best."

"Thank you, that means a lot." Suddenly, she swept me up in a hug. I flinched at first, but I accepted it anyway.

"If you need anything, call me." She extended me a number written on a piece of paper. I pocketed it.

"Sure thing, have you made arrangements and all that to get home?"

"Yup, don't worry about me, you've been more than fair." We left after that and I got home, feeling better than I had in a long time. I made a point of putting Chloe's number in my contact list and I texted her, saying if she ever needed anyone to talk to, I was there. She told me that was so sweet of me and that she would. I was just about to put the matter out of my mind when Chloe texted me a picture.

"I forgot to bring this. The woman on the left is the woman I saw with Allison's father that night."

I almost dropped my phone when I saw the photo. Suddenly, it felt harder to breathe and I had to hold onto the wall for a moment for support. After a few minutes, I managed to calm myself down enough to answer the message. Chloe immediately called me back and I told her what was up. She said if I needed anything, I should get ahold of her ASAP. I told her to come over tomorrow and we would get some answers.

The photo was older and a little faded. From the looks of it, it was taken in the late 80's, early 90's. There were two people in the picture; a woman and a man. The woman in it was an attractive brunette in her early 20s with a slender figure. From the looks of it she was happy, because a smile was plastered on her face for the picture. In the years since the photo had been taken, she had aged considerably and her style was quite different, but I still recognized her immediately.

Mrs. Arlington.

8

After I spent a restless night alone with my thoughts, Chloe arrived promptly at 2 pm. While she was right on schedule, it still wasn't fast enough for me. I spent the entire night going through everything I knew about Mrs. Arlington. I don't think I slept for a moment. Not even a shot of whiskey did the trick, but it did help calm me down a bit. Since it was a Saturday, we knew Mrs. Arlington, if that was even her real name, would be home.

I couldn't believe it. Did she know all this time? Was it a coincidence she moved next to me? Is that why Allison broke in? Not to get at me, but for a crack at her?

The last thought sent a shiver through my body. Right as if on cue, the doorbell rang. Not gonna lie, that moment made me jump. I ran to open it and there was Chloe. She walked inside without saying a word, but once the door was shut, she immediately greeted me with a hug. As is often the case, I didn't know how much I needed one until that moment. Sitting down on my couch, we tried to figure out how to approach the situation.

"I'll invite her here," I began. "I want her right where I know where everything is. My man John who I told you about will be here in a few too. Not gonna take a single chance. He'll be ready with some 'assistance' should it be required. In fact, another friend of his will be bringing some 'assistance' as well." Chloe nodded in approval.

"Good idea."

"I'll be the one to show her the photo and you'll tell her how you got it. We'll see where it goes from there."

"Sounds like a plan." She hesitated a moment before continuing. "What do you think she will do?"

I sat there for a moment, unsure of what to say. The woman had been an ideal neighbor for the entire time I had known her, not once had she done anything suspicious. She had been nothing but helpful and kind to me. At this point, she was almost like family to me. Perhaps part of me didn't want to believe anything bad would happen, but after everything that had happened so far, I wasn't about to count anything out.

"I don't know," I eventually whispered. John and his backup, another bouncer named Travis, got there about 45 minutes later. I didn't think it was possible, but Travis was even bigger than John was. But when he saw me, Travis immediately shook my hand.

"John told me what happened. Shit is crazy man." That was the most accurate thing anyone had ever said so far about this whole thing.

Shortly after they arrived, I called Mrs. Arlington to come over. I told her I had something I had to ask her about and to come over whenever it was convenient. As expected, she said she would be right over. When she spoke in her usual friendly, inviting tone, it made my heart sink. I know deep down she had a history I didn't know about, but I guess I didn't like the idea of ambushing her like this. But I immediately reminded myself I was doing the right thing and she had been the one keeping secrets.

"Just come on by now if you have nothing going on; the door is open," I made sure to keep my voice innocuous.

Mrs. Arlington immediately agreed and within minutes, I saw her walking across the driveway and up the steps. As the front door opened, I heard her call out and I told her to come into the living room. She walked into the living room and immediately looked confused.

"Oh, why hello there," she looked around at the people she had not been expecting. "Vince, I thought you had something to talk to me about?" Uncertainty penetrated her voice.

"I do," I said as I handed Mrs. Arlington the photo that Chloe had dug up. This was the original one, not some phone screenshot. I've always liked being able to hold an actual photo, especially on this occasion. She looked at it for a full minute, I think she was in shock. In that instant, you could feel the atmosphere change. It was like Mrs. Arlington was physically diminished.

"Where did you get this?" was all she could say. Her eyes looked different, more so than I had ever seen them; almost like a mouse's, timid and nervous. I didn't say a word, but I pointed to Chloe. I could see Mrs. Arlington nervously glancing at John and Travis.

"You were at Allison's house that night with her father. The bedroom. You both looked pretty keen not to be seen. Which makes sense, because he disappeared not too long after that. So please tell us what you know." In that moment, I could feel something silently break within Mrs. Arlington. If you have ever seen something bad happen to someone, you know what I mean. It is like their body physically changes before you.

"My God. I am so sorry I didn't tell you. I swear to you, I had no idea." She muttered before telling us more. "This was so long ago, I swear to you Vince, I had no idea Allison was Jerry's daughter. Goddamn it, it all makes so much sense. So, here is what I know. Damn, how could I have not seen the resemblance?" She cleared her throat thickly before getting down to business. "It's true, I was there that night. But not for what you think. As you know by now Vince, I used to be a legal secretary. One of the places I used to work was in Allison's hometown. Although it is only several hours away, it might as well be a million miles. I was fresh out of school and had just landed that job when Jerry Dunbar came to our office. Will Sanders was the best lawyer in town and it was an honor to work for him. I don't blame Jerry for wanting the best."

"What do you mean?" Chloe asked. Her brow furled in suspicion.

"You knew the Dunbar family?" Mrs. Arlington asked her.

"Yup."

"Then you know what I mean when I say things were not right in that family. Especially with the mother. It's why I say it all makes sense now. Jerry Dunbar came to us for legal help. He wanted a divorce from Allison's mother, Claire. But he didn't just want a divorce. No, he wanted full custody, and that was just a warm-up. Jerry said Allison's mother was dangerous and he wanted the courts to intervene."

I sat there silently, not sure what to feel. Chloe looked as pale as my kitchen floor, which was bone white. Mrs. Arlington's voice had become steadier as she spoke.

"He was terrified of her. Absolutely terrified. Over the years he had seen things, heard things, and when he was really lucky, he experienced it. For example, she would lie about the most routine things. Things no normal person would lie about. Or she would have an absolute fit over petty things. Like a piece of furniture being moved or the color of wallpaper. But she was never violent; at least not to him. That was one of the things that terrified him. She had all this aggression built up and very rarely, it would rear its head. But it would always go right away, leaving him unsure if it had really happened. Jerry's friend from work had a doctor for a brother, so one day Jerry asked for his opinion. Well, turns out Claire was a dead ringer for being ill, seriously mentally ill. I forget what it is called, but it wasn't bipolar or depression. No, this was major, as in 'call the FBI profilers' type bad. What's your name honey?" she suddenly asked Chloe.

"Chloe," she replied hesitantly.

"Lovely name," she said with a warm smile. In spite of everything, Mrs. Arlington managed to make Chloe smile as well. "Well Chloe, let me ask you something. Did you feel that Mrs. Dunbar was always perfect? Like a china doll that never gets blemished? Always had a perfect answer for everything?"

"Yes," she practically whispered.

"I had the same feeling too. Creepy isn't it? Almost makes you wonder if she was human. I didn't know exactly what to call it when I met her, but there was something different about her. Well, when Jerry called us, he said that he'd been thinking something was up for a long time, but what broke the camel's back so to speak was Claire's trip to visit her mother. The one that she took when you saw me at their house. Well, Jerry was instantly suspicious, because Claire LOATHED her mother, absolutely hated the woman. Called her every name possible and then some. So, when Claire started acting all concerned about her mother, Jerry knew instantly something was up. Once she was gone, Will had me go with Jerry to the house to look the place over. Said a woman's opinion was crucial. I would be able to look at things not just as an outsider, but as a woman examining another woman's habits. We looked for stuff related to Allison's grandmother, legal papers, letters, anything that would give us a clue to what was going on." Mrs. Arlington paused, a pained look then appeared in her eyes, as if she was bracing herself for something.

"Then we went into their bedroom. Which was where Claire kept her important papers, stashed inside a lockbox in her closet. That's why we went into the bedroom. I remember her closet was massive; filled with clothes, shoes in particular. It looked like she was trying to give Imelda Marcos a run for her money. Funny, now that I think about it, those two probably had a lot in common," she said to us as if she had just had some grand revelation. "But anyways, after some trying we managed to figure out the combination. For such a clever woman, she was surprisingly unimaginative about codes. It was Allison's birthday."

11.3.88. The number flashed through my mind like an involuntary spasm. I still remembered what I got her last year for her birthday: a new leather jacket. It cost an obscene fortune, but she looked so sexy in it. Light crème colored leather, I can still practically smell it. In spite of everything, the memory still managed to make me smile. Not that I would admit that to anyone.

"We opened the box and went through the papers inside. Inside was the usual; birth certificate, other identification papers, a few precious mementos, and other ordinary things. We were just about to put it back when Jerry found something. A recent life insurance policy had been taken out, but not for one of them, but for Allison's grandmother. Claire had taken it out about 6 months ago and had been steadily spending more time with her mother since then. The policy was for 450,000 dollars in the event of her mother's death. Bear in mind, Allison's grandmother was only in her early 60s and was in good health at the time, so it wasn't like she was betting on a sick old woman that would die at any moment."

At that moment, I felt sick. My intestines felt like someone was twisting them into balloon animals. It couldn't be possible.

"Confident that this explained a lot, Jerry told me he would get more information and speak to both me and my boss as soon as he had it. He kept in touch with us periodically, but never had any news. Finally, Jerry came to see us at the office a few months later. Didn't call or anything, he just barged right in. That wasn't like him at all. The man was always a stickler for etiquette, so we knew something was going on. He told us all that he was onto something and was gonna head out of town to follow Claire when she went to visit her mother this time. Allison was staying at a friend's house, so she didn't need to be watched. Jerry added that he would call us as soon as he could and with that, he left. Well that call never happened. He never came back and was reported missing three days later. But that wasn't even the worst part; the worst part was when the calls began."

"The calls?" I asked blankly.

"At first they came slowly. To Will Sanders at the office. No one ever spoke, just some heavy breathing. At first, we thought nothing of it. Working in a lawyer's office, you tend to become a bit desensitized to weirdness. But then they began happening at Will's home. Will had seen it all, so he could care less. Or at least that was the impression I got. But then they began happening at my house. At night. When I was alone, which was most of the time. At first, it was just more heavy breathing. Don't get me wrong, that was a bit creepy, but I could deal with it. But then someone spoke on the line, just one time. I will never forget that voice. It was a quiet voice, a charming sounding man. 'Don't worry about Jerry, if you know what's good for you. Unless you want us to check up on you. Especially if you go into houses that aren't yours again'."

I felt goosebumps pop up on my skin when Mrs. Arlington said this. I had never in my life seen her look so afraid. Just thinking about it seemed to terrify her.

"After that the calls stopped. They never called anyone else in the office but Will and me. To this day, I don't know how they knew I was with Jerry, but they did. Believe you me, I never went anywhere near the Dunbar house again. We told the police what happened, but they couldn't find anything. I left town not too long after that and did everything to forget the whole thing ever happened. I swear to you Vince, I had no idea Allison was Claire's daughter. I knew the girl's name was Allison, but there are a million Allison's out there. The few times I saw her she looked nothing like her mother. But it all makes sense now; they say if you want to see what a girl will be like when she gets older, look at her mother. This is the last thing I have to say; I have seen plenty of darkness in my life, but no human being ever made me look over my shoulder the way Claire Dunbar did."

We sat there in silence after Mrs. Arlington finished speaking. She stood there, her arms folded against her chest. I wondered how long she had kept this story to herself. Years probably. There were a million questions running through my mind. But somehow, Chloe asked the most important one before I could.

"What happened to Mrs. Dunbar?" Mrs. Arlington took a breath before answering Chloe.

"No idea, and I can't say I'm sorry for that. Most I ever heard is that she left town and no one heard from her again."

"Anything else?" I asked Mrs. Arlington blandly.

"No Vince, and I promise you, had I known that Allison was Claire's daughter I would have told you immediately." I sat there on the couch, thinking carefully about what I wanted to say.

"Thank you, that's all I wanted to know, Sharon." Her face fell instantly at this. But she nodded in response.

I had never called her by her first name before. It's sort of like a parent calling a child by their full name. That's when you know you are in deep shit. Without saying a word, she walked out of my living room. The door shut quietly behind her. I don't think she will be invited here any time soon. I thanked John and his friend for coming and they left shortly after. Chloe and I sat there for some time before she spoke.

"Do you believe it?" I nodded my head. I actually did believe her and I didn't need to ask Chloe if she felt the same. I could see it on her face that Mrs. Arlington had accurately described what Chloe had experienced when she lived next door to Allison. We had some answers now, but that just created about a thousand new questions we had yet to answer. Chloe walked to the door and told me she would keep an eye out and to call me if I needed anything. Now it was just me and my thoughts. One question dominated all the others. Odds were good Allison's father was dead.

But what happened to her mother?

9

After Chloe left, I was alone in my apartment. I took a deep breath and ran my fingers through my hair, reminding myself that really just happened. It's not every day you find out your neighbor knew someone your ex's batshit crazy mother. As I paced in my living room, I felt a wave of exhaustion suddenly wash over me. It's like that feeling when you're stuck on your feet all day and you finally get to sit down. You don't notice it in the heat of the moment, but it hits you later when you aren't expecting it.

It felt like a century had passed since I first met Allison. Hell, the more I thought about it, the less real it all seemed. It was almost too absurd to believe. I collapsed on the couch, stretched out, and put my feet up. But like I usually do when laying on the couch, I eventually turned on my left side so that I was staring at the carpet, but I wasn't really seeing it. After all this time, I didn't know what I believed about Allison anymore.

That's the sad thing about breakups; you wonder what happened and how things got to the point they did. But here's the dirty little secret; the person you first start dating isn't the same person you break up with. The person you fall in love with is them on their best day, the person you break up with is them on their worst day. Infatuation occurs when you see someone as the person you imagine they are. The breakup invariably happens when you realize that isn't how they really are. Hence what makes the end so painful at times; they weren't just lying to you. You were lying to yourself.

Think of it this way; the beginning and end of a relationship is a lot like ordering food. The version that's advertised looks delicious, appealing, and interesting, so you immediately order it. But how it actually looks and tastes when you get it is somehow different. Sometimes it's the wrong thing entirely, and if there is one thing I know, it's how infuriating it is when they fuck up your order. That's a breakup for you.

Did I ever really process the breakup with Allison? I don't even know anymore. Could it have gone another way? I have no idea. Did I do anything wrong? I had asked myself that question a million times, but I still don't have an answer. Was it my fault she went insane or whatever the hell happened to her? No, it wasn't. I knew that long ago, but Chloe's visit made it beyond obvious. Clearly, Allison had more baggage than an airport terminal.

It was all so weird, though. Times were good with me and her, or at least that's what I thought. Things went bad so quick I still can't quite get it. But that's what happens I suppose. I mean don't get me wrong, I wish things had ended on a different note between Allison and me. But I have no idea how that would have been possible. Another curse of dating I suppose. You don't realize how little you know someone until it doesn't matter anymore.

I still have no idea who Allison really was. But I don't think anyone else who knew her does either. One thing was clearer now; the girl had a royally screwed up childhood. It gave me chills just thinking about it. The worst part about this isn't what I know, although that's bad. No, the worst part was knowing that little bit, but also being aware there was more to the story and trying to imagine what else had happened. What I knew was just the tip of the iceberg, and the tip of an iceberg can do a lot of damage. Just ask the captain of the Titanic.

Trying to get that charming thought out of my head, I switched on the TV. After flipping through the channels, I didn't find anything that impressed me, so I decided on a movie; one of my all-time favorites, *Amadeus*. Arguably one of the greatest movies about jealousy ever made, it was always enjoyable to watch. After flipping through my DVR, I pressed play and turned up the volume. I let myself be taken to 18th century Vienna for a few hours. The stunning music and brilliant sets are always a wonder to behold.

After it was over, I decided to go out for a jog in the park. I've been doing it on and off for years when the weather is decent. After a day like this, I sure needed a run to help burn off some energy. After switching the TV back off, I changed into my running clothes and jumped in the car. The short drive to the park where I jog helped me relax. The area was well populated and still light out, so it was perfect. Parking the car, I began my jog. I started out slow, but soon I felt myself speeding up and I went with it.

Running in the crisp, cool air felt so refreshing. I did my usual circuit; 30 minutes plus a warm up and cool down. Towards the end, I panted as I felt my body burning up against the brisk mid-spring air. Cracking open my water bottle, I gulped about half of it down immediately. Water never tastes so good as when you are parched after a workout. I slowly walked back to my car and once I unlocked it, I sprawled out in the driver's seat. The only thing that is almost as good as water after a workout is when you get to sit down after it's over. As I drove home, I decided on what to have for dinner; roasted chicken with sautéed vegetables.

As I pulled in the driveway, I felt my appetite begin to take over. Getting out of the car was a bit of an effort, I felt that usual post work-out combination of satisfaction and fatigue. While mentally preoccupied making a list of the ingredients I already had, I grabbed my mail and began rummaging through it. Nothing but the usual stuff; a bill here and there with an ad thrown in for good measure.

There was only one other thing, a small envelope with my name written on it. There was just a single piece of white paper inside, folded in half. Using a black sharpie, someone had drawn a simple game of hangman. From the looks of it, the game was over, as the hangman stick figure was fully drawn. At the bottom where the word or phrase was, six spaces were drawn using thick black slashes. Someone had also filled in the letters above the lines.

D-A-N-I-E-L

What the hell? Who would send me this? I immediately grabbed the envelope; the label was typed on, innocuous, and professional looking. I grabbed my phone and called Chloe. Thank God she picked up immediately. As I heard her voice, it felt like my heart was racing almost as fast as when I was jogging.

"Hi Vince, what's up?"

"I got something in the mail. I'll send you a picture of it." I replied as I angled my phone for the best view of the hangman. She paused for a moment before she received it.

"That is disturbing looking," was all she could say.

"I know. I have no idea who Daniel is."

"I can't think of anyone either. So this is the second time someone sent you a little gift regarding being hung at the end of a noose."

"Third. I got a letter shortly after the first telling me next time the version of me at the end of a rope wouldn't be a doll."

"Damn. Ok, so clearly this is all connected somehow."

"Right, just let me think about it. I'll call you back as soon as I have more."

"Ok, and Vince? Be careful."

"I will." I ended the call and paced around my living room floor as I repeated the name Daniel in my head. After furiously racking my brain, I decided that the best remedy was to do something unrelated to stimulate thought. Since I was hungry and needed to eat something after my run, I decided that was as good as anything. Besides, they don't call it brain food for nothing. After taking the chicken out of the freezer, I preheated the oven, prepped the chicken, and tossed it in to cook. I made swift work of the vegetables; dicing up garlic, carrots, asparagus, and potatoes and tossing them into the pan. The simple and crisp smell filled the kitchen. Once the chicken was done, I took it out of the oven and checked it. Perfectly done, it was falling apart. Time to dig in.

While I shouldn't have been hungry after getting yet another disturbing thing in the mail, I have to say that at this point, nothing really phased me anymore. Not to mention I was no good on an empty stomach. I grabbed a plate out of the cupboard and immediately began devouring my dinner. It tasted amazing. The juicy chicken mixed perfectly with the crisp, flavorful vegetables. Being a pretty fast eater even without a workout, I was done rather quickly. Like most people, I always try to eat well after a workout. Otherwise you might end up needing a doctor or something.

Wait just a second. Doctor? That made me remember something. I grabbed my laptop and searched for something while I called Chloe back. When she picked up, I didn't wait for her to say anything before I began talking.

"Daniel. The guy who worked at the place where they took Allison. He took that bear of Allison's and died in a house fire not too long after."

"Just found it here too," she added. "Daniel indeed."

"I guess that means we may need to pay a visit to his family. See what he saw at the hospital."

10

I took a deep breath as I stepped off my front porch. The air was still thick with the scent from the heavy rain we had gotten earlier. I wasn't quite sure how I felt about this. I knew objectively I needed to do it, but the idea gave me absolutely no pleasure. None whatsoever. Here I was, taking time from my day off to go and dig up who knows what regarding Allison. I've heard of not being able to let someone go or move on after a break up, but this was downright absurd. At this point, bawling my eyes out while listening to Alanis Morissette looked downright amazing to me.

Come on. The sooner you figure this out, the sooner it will all be over, I told myself. It was a mantra I had been repeating to myself lately. While it didn't quite make me feel better, I knew it was the truth. I walked towards my garage and stepped inside; the pungent, earthy smell was oddly calming. Opening my car door and getting inside, I felt focused.

A car is your second home. Or perhaps your first depending on your living situation. One typically spends the bulk of their day in three places; work, home, and your car. Since what may be going on at one or two of them might be particularly unpleasant, it's always good to make sure the third is always in tip top shape. A well-kept car is the perfect way to help you relax and get down to business. I suspect it's one reason why road rage is particularly contagious; dealing with other drivers can puncture the temporary reprieve driving offers us. They joke about barbers or hair stylists knowing everything, but I will tell you who really knows all; limo drivers or any kind of chauffer. Know why? Because not only do they get to hear everything, but they also see it with their own eyes. It's one thing to hear about a crazy party, but actually witnessing America's Sweetheart snorting cocaine off a car's armrest on the way to a movie premier is very different. You think it's bad being the DD for your drunk friends on a Saturday night, that's like a boring Tuesday morning for a limo driver. They even made a movie called *Baby Driver* based on that idea and it was a pretty good one.

I turned the car on, hit the button to open the garage door, and cruised out of my garage. My car was particularly important to me these days, because it had been parked at work when Allison first dropped by with that little souvenir for me. The fact that she hadn't been able to touch it shouldn't have meant so much to me. But it did. Pulling out onto the road, I looked at the dashboard. It was 11 a.m., meaning I was right on time to pick up Chloe. Since we last spoke, I had been doing my own research on the guy who died in the fire. Nothing came up, nothing noteworthy in the news, no criminal record, just the little blurb about what happened. After about 15 minutes, I arrived at the hotel Chloe was staying at; The Walton Arms, one of those cheap but still moderately respectable inns. She was ready for me by the hotel's front, just as I expected.

"Hey, how are you?" she asked breezily as she hopped in the passenger seat beside me.

"Fine, I guess. Can't complain. You?"

"Good. Did you find anything?"

"Nothing. Not a single thing," I said as I pulled out of the parking lot and headed onto the highway.

"I didn't expect you would. I looked everywhere and from what I can tell, the dude was actually pretty boring."

"Yes, which totally explains why he took the teddy bear belonging to a dead girl and brought it home."

"Good point."

As the car glided onto the highway, I realized something. Chloe was the first girl to ride in my car since Allison. It wasn't an unpleasant thought or anything, but it was weird to think about. Putting it out of my head, I focused on the road.

"I know, it's so weird. But hey, that's nothing new. I can't wait to see what the doctor has to tell us."

"Ah, right. The doctor who told you Allison died in the hospital."

"Yup. I've always wondered what Allison did in the meantime after we broke up. The guy already spoke to me once when he didn't have to, so let's see if he'll do it a second time."

"Sounds like a plan." We went along in comfortable silence for a little while, the car humming on the road never ceased to help me focus. After a while, I thought of a question I had never really considered before.

"What kind of men did Allison go out with before me?" I threw a sideways glance at Chloe, she looked unsure of what to say.

"I don't really know. I remember that growing up she had the biggest crush on Justin Timberlake and her favorite Disney prince was Eric from *The Little Mermaid.*"

"So basically every other girl in the history of the universe," I muttered.

"Right. But I was always more of an *Aladdin* fan," she offered.

"I can respect that. Robin Williams made that movie what it was."

"He sure did. Fucking shame what happened to him."

"Is it bad that what happened to him made me sadder than what happened to Allison?"

"Did it?"

"You bet. Robin brought happiness to millions of people despite being in such pain himself. I felt like I personally knew the man. Allison, well, even though I spent plenty of time with her, I never really knew her. Even now, I don't have the faintest clue of who she was or what was up with her."

"That's understandable. Cheating cuts so deeply because it reminds us that we didn't understand or know the person as well as we thought. But that's not your fault. Let's try to get some answers, that's why I'm here," she added firmly.

We arrived at the hospital about fifteen minutes later. I stared for a moment at it, unsure of what to think. On the outside, it seemed like a respectable enough place; all properly maintained and whatnot. But it still gave me the creeps. We walked inside without saying a word to each other.

"Can I help you?" The orderly manning the front desk inquired of us. I could feel her eyes lingering upon us, trying to feel us out.

"Yes, we are here to see Dr. Edwin Burton," I answered her. She seemed to relax a bit at this. "Please tell him Vince O'Malley is here to speak with him."

"One moment, please." She stood up and hustled down a hallway and around a corner before she was out of sight.

I took the moment to take the place in. The entryway was a cross between a standard hospital and a government building. It had the same white, sterile, sanitized aesthetic you get in a hospital, but right alongside that was the official vibe of a social services department or courthouse. It was complete with security cards, cameras, metal detectors, punch pads, and Plexiglass windows. I bet everyone who works here gets plenty of smartass comments from their friends or whatever about their job. Personally, I bet working here wouldn't really be that different. Most of us work with lunatics, at least here you can identify them. As a bonus, they also give you a means of keeping them under control.

As if on cue, the orderly came bustling back towards us, the red and black lanyard holding her I.D. bouncing back and forth on her chest in rhythm to her steps. From this point of view, I could practically feel the fatigue coming off her in feeble waves, like the way a janitor here might wipe up a spilled liquid. Her eyes had the faraway, distant look that seemed to look at you for a second before moving right past you. Her frizzy blond hair was partially set in a tangled knot at the base of her neck in a futile attempt to tame it. Her hasty steps were masking the deep fatigue that would set back in the instant she retook her seat.

"Go right on in. Last door to the right, open for you." I faintly saw her badge had the name Virginia stamped on it, right below an unsmiling profile picture. Virginia pressed a hidden button by her station and the door popped open for us, announcing itself with a loud click.

"Thank you," I said gratefully.

The quiet reverberated around us as we walked down the hallway. Sometimes nothing was more deafening than silence. I can't say how Chloe felt, but I didn't like it. I have no problem with quiet or even silence, but this wasn't natural. It was like the silence when the power goes out; a suffocating state of mind more than a lack of sound. We were surrounded on both sides of the hall by doors with no windows, complete with small nameplates on them that I couldn't make out. Walking up the hall, I felt like an intruder wandering somewhere he didn't belong. Part of me wondered if that was what ran through Allison's head when she arrived. The other part of my mind promptly spoke up to remind me that when she arrived here, Allison probably didn't remember her own name, much less where she was. But then how would she have been able to get those pills inside? Time to ask someone with answers. To my immense relief, we were finally at the door to Dr. Burton's office.

I gingerly rapped on the door to announce our presence.

"Come in," the quiet voice replied. He sounded just like he did on the phone.

Upon crossing the threshold, I could see he was a professional looking man in his mid-50s or early 60s, with sharply trimmed salt and pepper hair.

"Hello Dr. Burton, it's Vince O'Malley. We spoke on the phone a while ago regarding Allison Dunbar," I said as I stretched out my hand by way of formal introduction. He immediately grasped it and shook it firmly.

"Yes, I remember. What brings you down here and who may I ask is this?"

"This is Chloe, she used to know Allison too and we thought you may be able to help us more than you already have."

"Lovely to meet you," he greeted her politely. "I'll do whatever I can to help you both," he finished before straightening the knot of his burgundy tie. On the coatrack behind him was a black suit jacket and a white lab coat. His office reminded me of a few of my colleagues; filled with books and papers, but still somehow creating the impression of order. Order and rationality amidst chaos, the best message to send in a place like this.

"So, we have been looking into Allison's past and apparently her mother would be in good company here." Dr. Burton furrowed his brow at this.

"I suspected as much. It's quite common in cases like hers."

"Yeah, and apparently my neighbor knew her family as well. It looks like Allison's mom made Allison's dad disappear. What exactly was wrong with her?" I could hear his desk chair creak as he leaned back in it.

"Well, since you are a person who is involved in the matter and the patient is dead, which means I can wave confidentiality, I will tell you both what I know and what I suspect."

"Thank you." I wasn't expecting to be quite so relieved when he said that.

"Can I get either of you coffee?" he offered as he was about to take a sip from his own cup.

"No thanks."

"I'm good, but we appreciate you offering," Chloe agreed.

"No problem. Well, here it is. Allison had some sort of psychotic breakdown not long after the two of you broke up. She cheated on you, correct?"

"Yes,"

"Right. Well, here is what I know. People with underlying issues don't just one day snap for no reason. Something inside Allison gave out while you two were still together. The breakup merely amplified it. Which is when she decided to let herself into your home and leave a little calling card. I don't need to rehash it, but all of her symptoms were that of a psychotic episode."

"Right. So that's what you know?"

"Correct." Dr. Burton laced his fingers together before sitting up straighter at his desk.

"What is it you suspect?" At this, Dr. Burton stood up hastily. He quickly walked past us and looked out his office door before shutting it. When he had resumed his seat, I saw he looked uneasy. Great. When someone who deals with batshit crazy on a daily basis looks uneasy, it's code for brace yourself.

"I presume you heard about the man who died in a fire?"

"Yes." When I heard my own voice I couldn't believe it. It sounded harsh, like I had just swallowed a jar of nails.

"Well, some of us were keeping an eye on him. He would have never helped Allison get the pills to hurt herself, quite the opposite in fact. We suspect he was behaving inappropriately with her." He enunciated the word 'inappropriately' slowly, like he was walking on eggshells, so each syllable was emphasized.

"He was screwing her?" Chloe asked abruptly. She was sitting stiffly in the other chair in front of Dr. Burton's desk, hands tightly gripping the chair's arms. If you didn't know better, you would think she was a patient.

"If it wasn't consensual, it would be sexual assault. But we have no reason to think it wasn't consensual. Let me tell you something. Working here, you have to pay attention to every detail. After enough time, it becomes second nature. You learn to read not just the patients, but their visitors and those who attend to them. I saw how Millstone looked at her. Plus, Millstone wasn't himself after she died."

"Got it. Well it seems someone else knows something. Because I just got a little something in the mail. Someone drew a hangman game with the name Daniel as the word to spell. It's the second time a hanging man has been left at my house." Dr. Burton looked shocked at this and didn't say anything for a few moments. I wasn't surprised. I suspected there wasn't really a course for this in med school.

"Wow."

"I also know he took that stuffed bear of Allison's. The one that she used to smuggle the stuff."

"Ah, yes. Well, I won't allow you to leave here empty handed either. As you can imagine, we keep a very close eye on who visits here, so I shall give you the records of anyone who visited Allison in that time; name, address, all the info you need."

"Thank you, that's very helpful."

"There is one last thing." His voice had dropped to a near whisper. "Be careful. I suspect that this wasn't the first time that bear was used to smuggle something. I told you I would be doing my own looking around, and while I haven't found anything concrete, something just isn't right. There is a reason she was so close to that thing. You saw her apartment, she was clearly afraid of someone."

"We will do our best. Thanks for everything, doctor." He stood up again to shake my hand as a farewell gesture.

"You're welcome, it's only fair. Oh, and Vince," he added as I was about to walk out.

"Yes?"

"She never once said anything bad about you here. Not once. Not when the police took her in, not when they committed her, and not once to a professional here." I had no idea how to feel about this.

"Ok." I couldn't really think of anything else to say.

"Do with it what you will. I just thought you should know."

"Wait," I suddenly thought of something. He paused as he was about to sit down, looking up expectantly.

"Yes?"

"Where is she buried?" What happened to the body?" The words came out of my mouth before my mind was able to process what I said. Somehow, the question sounded odd to my ears.

"Some relative claimed the body. Her cousin if I recall correctly. I know she was buried at a mausoleum called Heavenly Gardens."

"Thanks for everything, doctor."

"Of course, if you need anything else don't hesitate to call or visit." He picked up the phone and briefly instructed the front desk to give us the visitor records he mentioned earlier. With that, we walked out without saying a word. As our shoes clicked quietly on the polished floor, I was alone with my thoughts. I had never thought about what was done about Allison's body, and I had certainly never even considered what her grave was like.

Virginia at the front was ready for us with a handful of papers.

"Here you are," she replied politely as she handed them to me. "Shall I buzz you out?"

"Please." The door slid back open. I felt like we were leaving some sort of medieval castle that had just lowered the drawbridge for its visitors.

"Have a good day," Virginia bid us as we walked into the sunshine.

I took a deep breath as I felt the light wash over me. You don't realize how pleasant fresh air is until you are stuck breathing that chemically induced sanitized smell. A hospital or any sort of medical facility is one of two places with a distinct smell; the other is a shopping mall. At times, there isn't much difference between the two, particularly around the holidays. As someone who once worked at a department store during the holidays, people probably behave better at the psych ward. Not to mention this place is meant to bring sanity back; the mall exists to create insanity.

Clutching the papers tightly in my hand, I unlocked the car for Chloe and we drove off in silence. Not uncomfortable silence, just the natural absence of any conversation. We were both alone with our thoughts. In what seemed like no time at all, I arrived back at her hotel. She looked at it for a moment before getting out.

"See you soon, Vince. You know where to find me if you need me." I nodded in agreement and she walked away. At this point, we had developed a comfortable shorthand that didn't require intense explanations. As I pulled out of the parking lot, I felt myself relax. That unpleasant visit done, it was time to do some errands. It was something that always helped me process my thoughts.

†

I decided that since I had a rather challenging day, I'd earned a nice comfort meal, but not just any comfort meal; grilled cheese and tomato soup. Nor was it just any old grilled cheese either; because when making a legit grilled cheese, I use the same bread that I make french toast with. Just thinking about it on the way to the store made me feel better. After walking in and passing the greeting card section on the way to the breads, I noticed that they were having a clearance sale on out of season stuff. Amongst other items, they had one of those full sized plastic Santa statues on display. After I grabbed a fresh loaf of Brioche, I turned around and headed to the dairy. On the way, I saw the cheesy décor Santa again. While I didn't stop, I thought about it as I got the rest of the stuff I needed.

Why are these things always so sketchy looking?

I swear, I half expected Santa to be watching me as I walked away. We all heard the cliché urban myth about the clown statue and the babysitter growing up; but wouldn't a guy in a Santa suit be more realistic and terrifying?

Creepy Santa décor aside, I always enjoyed the holidays. But to be fair, I know why people hate Christmas or Thanksgiving. Because it's the two days of the year where people feel forced to be something they're not; a happy spouse, a loved family member, thankful, festive, cheerful, charitable, you get the idea. There is so much pressure to have the "perfect" holiday, but when it turns out to be not possible for whatever reason, it fills you with self-loathing, bitterness, and resentment; much like my Aunt Carolyn's yuletide fudge.

Relationships. Too many of them become like that Santa statue. Something you may have once found charming and fun only looks like bad taste in the end. As far as I could tell, the only difference between that sketchy Santa and Allison was that a teddy bear from Santa would be far less likely to cause bodily harm. A wry smile forced its way onto my lips at the thought. That creepy stuffed thing was the perfect symbol of my relationship with Allison; a harmless looking thing with something malignant lurking just beneath an appealing façade. No wonder why toxic relationships rip at people like a chainsaw. We finally realize the whole thing was a sick joke and we weren't in on the punch line. They are every asshole attempting standup at open mic night who somehow thinks they are humor incarnate, but everyone else just finds them obnoxious. In a toxic relationship, you start out being the rogue audience member who thinks their jokes are amazing, but slowly transform into the rest of the audience who eventually boos the wanna-be comedian off stage.

The only matter in question; how truly awful does the joke have to be before you decide the act is disgusting?

Also like hideous décor, you can only pretend that a person or bad relationship is fine for so long. It never fails that the moment finally comes when you cannot stand the sight of them for another moment and need to be rid of them. But once it is all gone, everything seems to return to normal.

Now it appeared like someone was trying to play a sick joke on me. Well I assure you, if I wouldn't let Allison herself do it to me when she was alive, someone using her in death would have about the same luck.

"Thank you," I told the cashier as he finished ringing me out. I walked out of the store with my bags in hand. As I was putting them in the trunk of my car, I kept thinking.

Without question, my biggest accomplishment regarding Allison is that the Halloween we were together, I managed to convince her to go as Morticia Addams when I was going as Gomez. I've always loved *The Addams Family*. The second Addams Family movie is perfect to watch for almost every time of year; Halloween, Summer, Valentine's Day, and especially Thanksgiving. If you've seen it, you know what I mean. The shade that Wednesday Addams throws in that movie is impressive. She's your favorite relative who sits at family functions with a glass of wine that is never empty and judges people. Everyone acts like they are always so mean, yet you never fail to smirk at their comments.

At first, Allison didn't want to go as Morticia. But that immediately changed when she saw how amazing she looked in the costume. I have to admit, that tight black dress looked spectacular on her. Now that I think about it, perhaps she got a bit too into the role. Between the two of them, Morticia Addams won in the normal department. The Dunbar family put the Addams clan to shame in the creepy department. Not to mention at least you would have a good time with the Addams family. That's what always made the Addams family one of the best family dynamics to watch. The only difference between them and the so called "normal" people they were thrown into situations with was that the Addams family never tried to hide who they really were. Most people have a morbid side; a hidden little thing they try not to bring out in polite company. Not only did the Addams family not try to hide theirs, they openly put it in display and reveled in it.

How refreshing. It's why the thought of Allison doesn't unnerve me like it used to. Because the real her is on display at long last. Once someone can't hide or surprise you, they lose most of their power. For many, sanity is simply insanity biding its time. No, the only thing that bothers me anymore is how I was asleep in bed with her for countless nights; blissfully unaware and helpless. Perhaps that's why I wanted to go as Tish and Gomez; my subconscious talking to me? Dr. Burton said she never said a bad thing about me. I guess that is supposed to mean she really cared about me or something. If that was her caring about me, I can't imagine what it would be like if she hated me.

As I passed through a bit of fog, I remembered something Dr. Burton had said. The teddy bear might have been used to smuggle something before. How long had she been involved in stuff like this? I couldn't believe she'd have the foresight to crush pills up and hide them in a stuffed animal in case she was institutionalized. Especially with her completely losing her grip. Turning onto Grunwald Street, I thought about how Mrs. Arlington heard her that day. What would have happened if she wasn't home? Or I had come home without knowing she was there? The stuffed version of me was bad enough, I don't even want to think about what else could have happened.

Wait a minute. I hadn't thought about that thing in months. After I found it, I put it aside in the garage so I wouldn't have to look at it again. I felt a weight fall into the pit of my stomach as I began to think. What if the teddy bear wasn't the first time something was hidden inside a toy? My hands automatically tightened their grip on the steering wheel as thoughts began frantically churning inside my head. I had to check that thing. Why didn't I think of this sooner? I felt my blood run cold as I remembered something else. The thing had been opened when I found it. Punctured, like it had been hacked open or something. At the time, we all thought she had stabbed it or something just for the hell of it. But what if that was just so Allison or someone else could hide something inside?

After what seemed like an eternity, my tires screeched as I pulled into my driveway. I slammed the car door shut and ran into the garage. Shoving other things aside, I fumbled for where I put the stuffed Vince. After a few moments, I found it. This was beyond insane. Studying it for a second, I tried to figure out where something would be hidden. I felt around the doll's limbs, listening for the sound of paper crinkling, or the texture of something that didn't match.

It took me about two minutes before I felt something. Right in the center of the doll I could feel something smooth, but solid. Tugging on the cuts in the doll, I ripped them open further. Tossing the stuffing aside, I found what was hidden. A small black plastic cylinder approximately the size of your pinky finger.

A flash drive. I felt myself swallow harshly. Allison, or whoever was here that day, wasn't just randomly here to trash the place. That's why nothing else had been touched.

11

I immediately went inside and plugged the flash drive into my laptop. I had no idea what to expect; there could be literally anything on here. I drummed my fingers impatiently on the keyboard as I stared at the screen, silently cursing it to load faster.

The contents eventually popped up in a window. There weren't any real names for files; they were only marked by numbers going from 1 to 10. I clicked the first one and saw it contained a video file. When I pressed play, my computer went into full screen video player mode. I took a deep breath and braced myself.

The first thing I saw was a shot of Allison's bedroom. From what I could tell, I was viewing things through her computer's webcam, because it was sitting on the dresser. I had a clear shot of almost the whole room. As soon as I realized what I was looking at, a blur came rushing into the room; it was the occupant herself. Taking in the sight, I remembered that the last time I had seen her, it was on camera as well. Except this time, she wasn't alone. Not only did she have company, she was making out with some guy. Now, when I say making out, I mean hardcore. The last time I saw that kind of face sucking, I was watching *Alien*. But even that was less disgusting than this.

My skin suddenly felt searing hot. This couldn't be what I thought this was. But it was. Within what seemed like seconds, they were doing it. I couldn't stand calling it anything else. I felt like I was vibrating out of my skin. Clearly the two of them were having a wonderful time. The next thing I knew, my hand slammed down on the keyboard and stopped the footage. Unbelievable. The little bitch couldn't just cheat on me, harass me, and generally intrude on my life. She actually had to film herself with another guy and leave the footage at my house. I lumbered to the kitchen, my shoes slapping harshly on the linoleum. A blast of cool air greeted me as I opened the freezer. The ice cubes felt soothing in my sweaty hand as I dumped them into a glass, then topped it off with a healthy amount of whiskey. For every occasion, there is a drink that goes well with it; champagne is for celebration, wine is for date night, beer is for a night out with your friends, and whiskey is for when you just need a stiff drink. As I tossed it back, my throat burned.

I bet this would be one of the cases the cops used for stories whenever someone asked about the craziest things they've seen on the job. I could see it now; late night, dinner at some overpriced family restaurant, everyone feeling nice and mellow after a few beers.

"One time this guy's crazy ex-girlfriend broke into his house and all she did was leave some stuffed thing that looked like him. But then it turns out that inside of it was a flash drive of a video with her screwing another guy." That's the one to beat, folks.

I could be on one of those Lifetime specials about love gone wrong. Maybe I should look into it, I might be able to make a few extra bucks. As I poured myself another drink, I began to feel the old bitterness waking up inside me, like an animal that had been hibernating. Part of me was also pissed off that the guy was good looking. She didn't even do me the favor of banging a guy who was a step down from me. At least then I could have gotten an ego trip that she downgraded. But who was I kidding, she wasn't considerate in life, why would she be any different in death? Tossing back the rest of my drink, I got in touch with the cops and informed them what I found.

Telling them about it made me feel absolutely filthy. I had to repress the urge to hop in the shower and scrub off a layer of skin. The dispatcher responded in a polite tone that they would be there soon. In the meantime, I poured myself another drink and texted Chloe about what I found. Mercifully soon after I called, a single squad car parked in front of my duplex. I watched from my front door as a suited detective climbed out of the driver's seat.

"Thank you for calling us, Vince," he said with an outstretched hand, "I'm Detective Ramsay." He was a middle aged, wiry man with green eyes that reminded me of a tie I once owned. A mild green, the kind that looks nice as icing on a cake. We shook hands briefly before I led him inside.

"Sure thing Detective, just get this thing out of my sight for good," I grunted as I shoved the flash drive and remnants of the stuffed toy at him. "Happy viewing."

"I know that had to be rough to see. We'll go through everything and keep you posted about what we find."

"I appreciate that," I replied as he put both items into a special kind of plastic bag.

"We officially consider Allison's death a suicide. No one is disputing that, but we do consider the circumstances of her death to be…. interesting, to say the least."

"Yeah?"

"Yes. We have everything you've told us, and we know about the paramedic. We are pursuing all leads, but we don't have much. If you find or hear anything else, give me a heads up." He handed me a business card that I put inside my wallet after glancing at it briefly.

"What do you think about him?"

"A paramedic who knows several languages and gets infatuated with a patient? Yeah, we definitely think there is more to it than that."

"Did you check out the stuffed bear?"

"Sure did. When Allison turned up dead, we ran tests on it and confirmed it contained residue of Oxycodone. It was also in Allison's system when she died. But after we did what we had to, we gave it back along with her personal effects for when someone claimed Allison's body. It seems Mr. Millstone eventually claimed it for sentimental reasons. You mentioned she had a history of substance issues?"

"Yup."

"Which substance or substances specifically?"

"Heroin and general opiates as far as I know for sure." I recalled as Ramsay jotted efficiently in his notebook.

"I'm gonna level with you Vince. I think she and Millstone may have known each other before. It was probably no coincidence she was committed to that hospital."

"Why?" My throat tightened uncomfortably as he spoke.

"A paramedic would have unprecedented access to heroin and countless other drugs. Around here, paramedics deal with heroin about as regularly as heart attacks. He wouldn't be the first to succumb to it, not by a long shot. It would also explain why Millstone paid close attention to her and why he made sure to get the stuffed bear."

"You think there was more in there than what Allison took?"

"Very good observation, that's exactly what we suspect. Millstone lived in a nice house, on a paramedic's salary, while his wife was a stay at home mom."

"Interesting,"

"It is also worth noting that he died in a fire without a trace of a break in or anything."

"Do you think she had anything to do with it?"

"Allison or Mrs. Millstone?"

"His wife, but at this point neither would surprise me,"

"It's possible. Insurance money is one motive. Not to mention she probably knew about her husband and Allison. Or suspected it, at least. I don't need to tell you how infidelity can be sensed, even if it's not a conscious observation."

"Got that right. Not to mention bringing home a dead girl's teddy bear is just weird."

"Well yeah, there is that. He may have also just wanted a token of grief or something. But that's all I have for now, Vince. Be sure to take care of yourself and call us if you need to."

Before I knew it, he was walking through the front door and I was by myself again. I felt exhausted, like all the nonsense of the last few months finally caught up with me. The girl on the tape was the Allison I remembered. Not some shell of a human being who was insane and drugged out of her mind. When you really get down to it, our romantic prospects are nothing but mysteries we hope to solve. 'Who is she? Does she have a boyfriend? Does she like me?' Dating is nothing more than an attempt to answer those questions and many more we will probably never get an answer to. But we want the answers bad enough that we keep trying.

But if you have the unfortunate privilege of having an unfaithful significant other, the appeal to play detective only gets stronger. So many people can't resist obsessively looking up the other woman or whatever on Facebook, frantically trying to see what they look like. Even people who haven't been cheated on will obsess over whose photo their fiancé liked and made a flirty comment on. The sad thing is, that's just a warm-up. What follows is going through their SO's phone, eavesdropping on their conversations, and micro-analyzing their every waking moment. This can happen even in relationships where both partners are faithful.

It reminds me of how back during the Cold War, there were experts on the Soviet Union called Kremlinologists. They would carefully study every single picture and speech of the top officials, taking careful note of who was in what pictures, who gave the longest speech, what speech got the loudest applause, who sat with who, and who seemed to be missing. All of this was in the hope of ferreting out where the true power resided and what the Soviets were truly up to. Modern relationships, particularly unhealthy ones, are based on a similar premise; two mutually suspicious parties fixated on what the other is up to. But at least during the Cold War people acknowledged how dangerous the situation was. It seems most people don't recognize a relationship is bad until it's over.

Speaking of recognizing something, to this day I have no idea who it was that Allison cheated on me with. Some people dream up this whole character in their head about who the person is. Not me. I like not knowing, because it means I could theoretically bump into him on the street, not recognize him, and just go right on with my day. Even when I first found out about Allison's bad behavior, I couldn't care less who it was with. I wasn't forming some long-term plan for revenge. The only thing that mattered was that it wasn't me. Looking into it will only drive you crazy with more questions you can probably never answer, the most common one being, 'Why them?' I never even asked for the guy's name. Which means I don't know if that guy from the video was the same guy from before, or just another name in a long line of hookups. Personally, I suspect the latter. Either way, it doesn't make much difference to me.

It took me a moment to recognize that someone was knocking on my door. Walking lazily towards it, I saw Chloe on the other side of the peep-hole. Interesting, I didn't ask her to come by. When I opened the door, she didn't say a word, but her eyes screamed "Holy shit, I am so sorry sweetie." I also noticed she was holding a large pizza box; the perfect offering for any occasion.

"I got garlic bread too," she added while gesturing with the pizza.

"Cheesy?"

"Damn right." I couldn't help but offer her a faint smile. This small mercy meant more to me than I ever expected. We sat down on the couch and watched old episodes of *Arrested Development*, one of my favorite shows along with *The Americans*. Chloe didn't say a word, but she sat quietly beside me and made herself comfortable. It was nice. After stuffing my face, I felt considerably better. After three episodes, I felt myself shifting on the couch towards her.

"Why exactly do you care about what happened to Allison? Better yet, how do you have the time to stay out here?" Before answering my questions, Chloe adjusted herself on the couch so that she was sitting with her legs folded underneath her.

"Like Allison's family, I grew up pretty comfortable. My family owns the patents for several pesticides along with some real estate. All I've ever really done is what I was supposed to do; go to the right schools, mingle with the right people, date who I was supposed to date, work within the family network. But it never made me happy. Not that it ever really makes anyone happy. I guess I felt like I failed Allison, because I felt like I had been failing myself for years as well. I think a lot of people failed her. But the best answer to that question is that for the first time, I feel like I am doing something meaningful. But aside from that, it's just interesting. The girl gets your attention just as much in death as she did in life."

"Good point." Another rich girl, I wasn't sure how I felt about that. I wonder if Allison was only friends with her because her family had money. That wouldn't surprise me one bit.

"Was I one?" I didn't elaborate, but I could tell she knew what I was asking.

"No, Vince, she was damn lucky to have you for as long as she did and what she did is unforgivable." I swallowed thickly at that. While people have told me that countless times, this one felt different. More real.

"Thank you." I smiled at her. I can't remember if I've ever smiled at Chloe since I met her. I made a mental note to do it more.

"Just the truth," she said quietly.

"Tell me more about the Dunbars,"

"What about them?"

"Everything you know. I don't think I've even asked you where you're from. How rude of me."

"It's ok," she added quickly. "I don't blame you. I did sort of butt into your life unexpectedly because of a crazy situation." She brushed a few crumbs off her jeans. I couldn't help but notice how tight her jeans were. It was a good look for her. "I am sorry about that."

"Don't worry about it. Without you, I would still be in the dark about a lot of stuff."

"That's kind of you to say."

"No worries. So where exactly are you from?"

"Maple Bluffs, it's just outside of St. Louis."

"Nice place?"

"It was once," she emphasized the final word with a forlorn look. "Years ago, it was a tranquil, good sized city. Now it's nothing but a shadow of its former self. Has one of the highest heroin rates in the state. Part of town is still nice. The other though, not so much."

"Pity. What else do you know about Mr. and Mrs. Dunbar?"

"They were your old school husband and wife. Mrs. Dunbar never really held a job as far as I know, but she didn't really need to either. Allison's grandfather was a doctor. The family also owned a newspaper and a meatpacking plant amongst other things. The paper was called the Gilford Gazette, I think. They sold it a long time ago."

"Ah, that explains Allison's fixation with gossip."

"Yup. But that's not to say Mrs. Dunbar was just some bland housewife. Not even close. She was the woman all the other women in town turned to. I can still remember her holding court in that old wicker chair out on their front porch; sweaty glass of tea or lemonade in one hand, clutching it with her burgundy nail polish. When she would emphasize a point, the ice would clink away in the glass to the rhythm of whatever she was saying. 'I just cannot wait,' clink, 'to get started on the bake sale,' clink," she finished in an exaggerated, honeyed voice.

"Charming,"

"She was also the chair of the women's committee and was on the PTA. She was known in town as The Duchess. Not to her face of course."

"Right,"

"But it definitely suited her. She had the ladies in waiting to go right along with it, her own little clique; Janet Halliday, Cindy McGinn, and Barb Fields. They would all go out regularly for brunch; eggs benedict washed down with a bloody mary or two.

"Naturally." I couldn't help but roll my eyes at this.

"Oh yeah, they were something alright. My mom went with them once and she hated them all, probably still hates them in fact. Mrs. Dunbar even had the cliché doll collection that she thought was charming but was really just creepy."

"I bet the dolls weren't even close to the creepiest thing in that house. Did she try dressing Allison like them?"

"Afraid so," she gave me a 'What can you do?' shrug. "But as you probably guessed, that didn't work out well. Allison threw A FIT about it and the next thing I knew, Mrs. Dunbar sold all the dolls."

"Good for Allison, she finally did something I can agree with."

"Yup. But you get the idea; a parent living vicariously through their child. Different generation, same bullshit."

"Exactly. She may not be homecoming queen or whatever the town has anymore, but her daughter is. That's totally the same thing, right?"

"Totally. But I am a bit surprised she didn't marry a man like her father."

"Wait, why?" I didn't know quite how to take that statement and had no idea if she was talking about me.

"Because I swear, any doctor could make their entire practice off Mrs. Dunbar. Every time you saw her, she had either just finished some checkup or was about to have one. Mrs. Dunbar would fuss over Allison about everything; 'Make sure you put on the sunscreen sweetie' or 'Don't eat too much salt, it can make you bloated honey.' That kind of thing."

"There is one of those per family." I leaned back against the couch, relieved that she was talking about Mrs. Dunbar. Taking my half empty glass of iced tea in hand, I took a big drink of it while Chloe kept on talking.

"I know. Especially considering she was a doctor's daughter. An old school one too."

"Ouch. Can't imagine how daddy worried about every little cough or cold. Faking it to get out of school is out of the question."

"Yeah, but I think the status made up for it in the end."

"Not to mention plenty of pills." She gave a silent nod of agreement. We sat there a little while longer before it was Chloe's turn to ask a question.

"How did you feel when you found out about Allison and the other guy?" That wasn't the question I was expecting at first, but I wasn't surprised either.

"Angry at first, but then just blah. Not depression, but like I had been hollowed out with nothing left inside."

"Why?" She crossed one leg over the other and leaned on the couch with her shoulder, facing me.

"Because deep down, I was always surprised she was with me."

"Too good to be true?" She ran a hand through her hair, sweeping it behind her with one deft wave.

"Sort of, but it was deeper. It was like something you enjoy in the moment but can feel it coming to an end. Know what I mean?"

"I do, it's like the end of a movie."

"Well said. But I just wish it hadn't ended quite like that."

"Course you do. Did you learn anything from being with Allison though?"

"Relationships are like jobs; you take a little something with you from each one, whether you realize it or not."

"This is very true. Some are better than others,"

"The little inside joke on people is that you really can't assess a relationship and it's impact on you until it's all over. It can even take years. But when you think about it, that makes sense. As you said, it's like a movie. You can't give a final, objective look until it's over and you can study the whole thing. Sometimes you might need to watch it more than once."

"So what is your final objective look on Allison?"

"Which Allison?" Chloe looked at me puzzled.

"What do you mean?"

"I mean which Allison? The one I first met, the one who cheated on me, or the one who wound up in the hospital? That's my verdict. I liked the Allison I first met, but she didn't last. That was just a pleasant façade that masked deeper issues."

"That's fair." She cleared her throat and leaned back on a pillow.

"She had major issues, it just took a little while for them to come out."

"That's right." Chloe nodded along in agreement.

"When I found out she was using, it was beyond question that something was seriously wrong with her, because people who are truly happy never use drugs; they don't need to. I don't mean prescription stuff for serious medical issues like diabetes or heart disease. I'm talking about people who use cocaine or whatever and pretend everything is amazing and drugs just come with the territory. That's about the biggest lie I've ever heard. They pretend they're happy, but it's nothing but a front. People take illegal drugs for the same reason they take legal ones; because something is up with them. It's just a question of what."

"Can't argue with that."

"Speaking of prescriptions, can I get you a refill?" I couldn't help but notice her glass of water was empty and she was tapping it absentmindedly with her fingers.

"Oh, no thanks, I'm fine. But please go on."

"Sure thing. Anyway, I've seen it all the time at work from students and faculty alike. I have yet to find a truly happy person who developed a drug addiction. It's why deep down, I wasn't surprised Allison cheated on me. Adultery is a lot like developing an addiction; people who are well functioning, truly happy, and content won't even consider it. People love to pretend that 'one thing led to another,' and they just so happened to wind up having sex with some person other than your girlfriend or whatever. Bullshit, there was a reason you did that, it's just a question of what it was."

"It's why we all have a limit. All of us have the potential to be unfaithful, the only difference is what would make us do it."

"Absolutely." I couldn't have agreed more. "You know, that's what always bothered me most."

"What bothered you the most?" She asked while rolling up the sleeves of her purple sweater.

"I never knew exactly why she hooked up with someone else. I could have cared less about who she did it with, but the reason why was a different story. The best answer I came up with was the same reason she got into drugs."

"Which was?" Chloe was looking at me, but she wasn't focusing on me alone. She had that look where you are thinking about more than the topic at hand, but I continued on.

"There was something going on that compelled her. Some need or urge she was trying to satisfy. Same reason people get prescriptions from the doctor; there is something going on that they can't address themselves, so they seek out something that can. Or something that they think will do the trick."

"Interesting association between addiction and bad relationships,"

"It's more than an association, the two are virtually the same thing. Think about it. Once you're with an addict, you are with someone who is eternally unfaithful. Their attention will always be elsewhere and they won't stop going behind your back for a cheap thrill. It may be with a flesh and blood person, a hypodermic needle, slot machine, a bottle, or a line of white powder. Doesn't really matter what. It's all the same idea though, an addict's most important relationship is with their addiction. Unless that changes, you will always be second to that. They will always be unfaithful to you." Chloe was now looking straight down at her feet.

"Can't argue with that. Addiction is the ultimate abusive relationship."

"Yeah."

"The ups and downs of relationships can be a lot like a drug and its aftermath. When you're up, you're up, but when you're down, you are really down. An upper and downer rolled into one."

Her gaze still hadn't moved from her feet. In all the time I'd known Chloe, I didn't think I've ever heard her talk about herself before that night. Not once. Time for that to change and change fast.

"Who was it?" I asked as gently as I could.

"Who was what?" That got her attention. She looked up and when she did, Chloe seemed so sad that it broke my heart.

"The addict." It was a statement, not a question. She sat in silence. I could practically feel the emotions surging through her, fighting for release. 'Do I tell him? Should I lie?' I was just about to drop it when she finally answered.

"My father." I think she was telling herself as much as me.

"Do you want to talk about it?' I offered, inching closer to her on the couch. Chloe took a deep breath before speaking in a quiet, but still firm voice.

"Let me put it this way; living in our house was sort of what I imagine living in a haunted house would be like. You can feel the malevolence always lurking, just waiting to make itself known, but you never quite know when it's going to jump out and get you."

"That's horrible." I had seen plenty of those movies myself. While I certainly enjoyed watching them, I can't ever say I'd want to temporarily be in one, much less experience it on a daily basis. I felt myself slide over even closer to her on the couch. Before I knew it, I had placed my arm around her and was rubbing circles into her shoulder. I had never seen Allison act even remotely as vulnerable as this girl. I felt awful seeing her like this, but it was nice to see a real human being processing genuine emotion for once.

"Thanks," she said gratefully. "My father is your usual rich alcoholic; people never openly referred to him as one, but you can bet they always made sure to lock up the liquor cabinet when he was around. If he had any brains or talent, he would be off doing something important. But nope, he is the family drunk who makes his brother and sister grateful. Because compared to him, their problems are virtually nothing."

"And your mom?"

"She's good." Chloe's voice had grown much stronger now. "She wasn't some rich woman with battered wife syndrome. Mom was the brains of them, the one with the head for business. In fact, someone once said that had she been born a man, there is no telling what she could've done. But that never bothered her, and she does pretty well for herself as it is."

"Good for her." She didn't come right out and say it, but I could practically feel the pride Chloe had in her. She scooted a little closer to me without saying another word. Before I knew it, I had drifted off to sleep.

12

I woke up slowly the next morning. At first, I forgot where I was. But when I realized Chloe was still asleep next to me, I remembered what happened. Taking in my surroundings, the digital clock on my DVR said 11:03. While trying not to wake her, I got up and grabbed my phone. I wanted to call and update Dr. Burton. On the third ring he picked up.

"Hello?'

"Hi Dr. Burton, it's Vince," I began.

"Why hello, Vince," his polite tone greeted me. "What can I do for you today?"

"I just wanted to give you an update. Inside the stuffed mini-me Allison left at my house was a flash drive. There was footage of her having sex with some guy on it." The silence on the call reverberated for several seconds. I imagined him sitting stunned at his desk.

"I am so sorry, Vince," I had never heard him use that tone before. Listening to it, you would have thought he personally failed me as a patient.

"Thanks. It is what it is."

"Vince?"

"Yeah?"

"Have you ever heard of oxytocin?"

"You mean OxyContin?"

"No, I mean oxytocin,"

"Can't say that I have."

"Well, oxytocin is a hormone your body makes. It's connected to feelings of love, sex, affection, and everything in between."

"Cool." I was wondering why he was telling me this. But part of me suspected he had a reason.

"It's called the love hormone and is key to all forms of human bonding, especially physical affection. You aren't the first person to confuse it with OxyContin. It's spelled very similarly."

"That is uncanny. The love hormone is spelled almost identical to an addictive pain pill."

"I know. Although from my experience the love hormone can be its own addictive drug."

"Good point. Just like heroin is spelled almost the same as heroine."

"It sounds exactly the same and there is only one letter separating the two; I've always found that rather unsettling."

"Instead of turning to a heroine, some people turn to heroin."

"Indeed. I couldn't help her, her father couldn't help her, and not even Millstone could help her. End of story."

"That is why I mentioned it, Vince. In my professional opinion, Allison suffered from a lack of proper development, coping skills, and sincere human relationships. I can't confirm it, but since her grandfather was a doctor and, from my research, had legal issues with morphine, odds are good the issue was genetic."

"That is helpful."

"Plus, those with mental illness are quite susceptible to addictive behaviors. So she was in double trouble as it were. Family history of both mental illness and substance abuse."

"Yeah, that's right."

"I just wanted you to know it wasn't your fault. I tried to help Allison too, but I failed." I had never thought of that before, but he was right. I suddenly felt an odd sympathy for the guy.

"Don't be too hard on yourself Dr. Burton. I guess now we have something in common huh?"

"We do indeed." Dr. Burton felt more familiar to me now; like we were both part of the club of people that Allison's past and bad behavior had affected. "Call me if you need anything else."

"Will do." I ended the call and tossed my phone on the kitchen counter.

Talking to Dr. Burton had actually made me feel better. While he was a psychiatrist, it still took me by surprise somehow. Funny, because not much was able to do that anymore. He had a solid point, too; love can often be found at the heart of most despicable things. But it's usually a love of something rather than someone; love of money, love of power, love of sex, love of drugs, and sometimes love of violence. In my experience, most substitute love of something for love of someone. Just look at what most people do when they go through a bad breakup; binge on junk food, alcohol, and perhaps some ill-conceived one-night stand.

While still standing in the kitchen, the idea of breakfast entered my mind. Today felt like a cereal kind of day. But before I could decide on which kind, my phone demanded my attention again.

"Hello, Vince? It's Detective Ramsay,"

"Oh hey Detective," I braced myself for whatever news he had.

"Just wanted to give you an update on what we found on the flash drive."

"Shoot."

"Well, there was a lot more to that recording than just what you saw. It seems after they had sex, things got a little rougher between Allison and him. A lot rougher."

"How much rougher?"

"The guy ended up dead. They started out just arguing and he got rough with her; tried choking her and everything. She fought back and got the best of him. We actually found the body a while ago. It was one of our cold cases that we can now mark solved. So whatever you might think of finding that footage, it was able to help solve that case." I felt the blood rushing to my ears and the room suddenly felt 20 degrees warmer.

"I guess that is something," I somehow managed to answer.

"The guy in question was Josh Marshall. Rap sheet goes on for a mile, lots of drug related stuff."

"Shocker,"

"I know. That's even how their fight started. We had a professional tech guy break down the audio and the argument began over drugs. The payment for their most recent score, to be exact."

"Charming. I guess the couple that scores together whores together." I felt a faint bit of pride over that rhyme.

"You have a point there. But there's plenty more where that came from. It appears Allison had some outstanding financial obligations."

"That's no surprise. The girl had no head for money; I'm amazed the bar she ran didn't go out of business. Not to mention good drugs are pricey."

"It was deeper than that. According to her bank records, she was withdrawing money at a suspicious rate."

"What are you telling me?"

"You said she was cheating on you, didn't deny it, and got defensive when you confronted her?"

"That's right. Who the fuck was I to tell her what to do or something like that."

"Well, Vince, I don't think she was cheating on you just for the hell of it," I felt my free hand not holding the phone tightening into a fist as I tried to focus. It was too early for this, I hadn't had breakfast yet, or even my coffee.

"Ok so, why did she do it exactly?"

"There is no easy way to say this, but we think Allison may have taken up a new side venture. Either prostitution or drug dealing."

"No way." Believe me, I had thought of Allison as a whore plenty of times before, but this was insane. She had actually become a hooker?

"The other option is that she was supplying his habit and they just hooked up for the hell of it. Personally, I tend to suspect that more."

"I would have to agree. I could see that far easier than the prostitution one. I always thought her guy on the side was the one giving her drugs."

"It's understandable Vince," Ramsay reassured me.

"But where was she getting it?"

"You know she managed a bar, right?"

"What about it?"

"I did some digging and the bar is actually owned by her family."

"No shit?"

"I have it right here in front of me; Claire Dunbar is the registered owner." The room felt like it had suddenly plummeted in temperature.

"How?" I heard myself breathe into the phone.

"I don't know, but I promise you I'll find out."

"Detective?"

"Yes, Vince?" A note of genuine concern filtered into his voice.

"Do you think someone deliberately tried to drive Allison crazy? Or was it just guilt over Josh?" The silence on the other end lasted longer than I expected. I even looked at the phone to make sure Ramsay was still on the line.

"I've considered that myself. Since both Allison and a paramedic known to be familiar with her have both died under odd circumstances to say the least, I think it's a good possibility."

"But why?"

"That's the million-dollar question, Vince."

"Does it have something to do with that bear?"

"I think so. It's one of the things that link them." Ramsay's voice had now dropped to a whisper like mine.

"What can I do?"

"Keep your eyes and ears open and your mouth shut. I'm gonna do some looking into that hospital and see if anyone else catches my attention. I'm also looking into Allison's friends and other acquaintances."

"Sounds good."

"One last thing. And please, be honest." His voice had dropped to the point where it was almost inaudible. "Did she do anything else to you besides cheat on you?"

"No. Nothing like that."

"Ok, good. Because if she did, I wouldn't want you to feel the slightest hesitation about telling me. This girl had major issues."

"I appreciate that, and you got that right."

"Very good. Eyes open and I'll keep you posted. Stay safe, Vince."

"You too, Detective."

There it was. She had actually killed someone. With a sick lurch, I remembered the last time I saw her, she thanked that stuffed thing for helping her get rid of some guy. I sat there in silence for a few moments. All this time, I wondered what she was truly capable of, and now I finally had an answer. I was torn. Part of me knew it had been in self-defense. But she had also invited that scumbag into her life to begin with. She had to have known what he was like. I suddenly remembered what they found at her apartment; the words 'He's coming for me' all over the place. Was she worried about someone coming to avenge Josh or something? Ramsay had a point; if someone was deliberately trying to make Allison go insane, they had to have a motive. Although I doubt she needed much assistance in the going insane department.

While trying to process what I was just told, I remembered that Ramsay didn't say when the guy died. I felt my heart plummet like a cinder block that was just dropped off a cliff. That footage was left here months ago. Meaning she had to kill that guy sometime before she let herself in. I had no idea if Josh was killed before she and I officially ended things, after, or anytime in between. Was that why she tried frantically contacting me? She could have wanted anything, a hand to get rid of the body perhaps. That would have been one hell of a conversation. *"Hey baby, I know we're broken up or whatever, but I could really use your help with something."*

In the next room Chloe was stirring on the couch. I could hear it's worn leather moving as she shifted and sat up. I turned out of the kitchen to face her, unsure of what exactly to say.

"What's up?" When she looked at me, I could tell she knew something was bothering me.

"Allison killed that guy I saw her with on the video. Some low-level drug guy who tried to strangle her. Was on the books as a cold case for a while." She sat there silently, seemingly unsure of what to say.

"We need to go see Mrs. Millstone," she offered out of nowhere after what seemed like forever.

"Let's not and say we did." I began to move back towards the kitchen, desperate for some coffee.

"Do you not want to?" Chloe sounded puzzled.

"What gave it away?" As I turned back around, I felt the bitterness from last night return with a vengeance. All Chloe did was look at me.

"I know it's not exactly the most appealing task, but to find out what happened to her, we need to know what happened with him."

"I am fucking sick and tired of her!" I shouted as I felt something snap inside me. "I broke up with her to get away from her and her bullshit. I was done with it and ready to move on with my life. But does she let me? Hahaha!" The laughter was caustic and harsh even to my ears. "I wish. It's been worse than ever. You know what? I had a life before Allison and I will have a life after her. But all you and anyone else knows me as is the guy she was dating. I'm sick of it. She's dead so she should just fuck off for good! " Chloe looked stunned at my outburst.

They love to describe anger as the color red. Seeing red. But anger isn't red. Red is a warm, engaging color. Full of life. If anything, black is more akin to anger; lifeless, dominating, all consuming. I felt my chest heaving up and down. I looked at Chloe again and she looked sad. Now I felt bad. She was a good person who I liked and didn't deserve that.

"I'm sorry," I mumbled out. I felt ashamed at my outburst. She didn't say a word but came over and wrapped me up in a hug. At first, I sort of flinched at her touch. Then I found her embrace comforting. Like a hot bath after a horrible day at work.

"It's ok. I've been expecting that for a long time. We are going out in the next couple days. You and me. No one else allowed."

"That sounds amazing. I'll pick you up at 6 and we'll go to a movie, then grab some food?"

"I'll be ready." she smiled widely. It was the first time I'd seen her genuinely happy since I'd met her.

13

After I made plans with Chloe, she headed back to her hotel and I was left with a ton to think about. I still couldn't believe that she seriously left footage of her killing a guy at my house. Is that what she really wanted me and everyone else to see? I don't even know anymore. But I know for certain she left it here at my house specifically. Not content with that, she left it in something that specifically looks like me. Subtlety never was Allison's strong suit. I guess irony wasn't either. Most couples usually end up arguing over the woman leaving harmless junk at the guy's house, trivial things like dental floss or makeup. I got homicide footage.

But I was most surprised at my own outburst. I felt suddenly winded, like I had sprinted on the last bit of a run. Deep down, though, I was really amazed it took this long for that to come out. Resentment and emotional baggage is like hoarding junk; you don't realize quite how much useless shit you have stored up until you start going through it. There isn't exactly a self-help book or something for this. At least not yet. But in this day and age, "How to cope with a psycho ex for beginners" would probably make a killing. Especially since you could make double the money if you wrote one version for men and another one for women.

I sat down on the couch and spent the rest of the afternoon reading a book with some bad reality TV on as background noise; one of those shows where a bunch of people live in a house and there's drama. When I was done reading, I decided to take care of something important. I tugged my phone out of my pocket and with a few deft movements, I dialed Mrs. Arlington's number. I wanted to do it quickly while I still had the urge.

"Hello?" The quiet question somehow caught me off guard.

"Hi, Mrs. Arlington, it's Vince." I hope I didn't sound as awkward as I felt.

"Vince! It's so good to hear from you. Is everything alright?" she asked immediately. I could hear the genuine concern in her voice.

"I guess so. I just had some more questions for you."

"Of course. I will be happy to help you as much as I can." I felt like there was something more I should say.

"I appreciate that. I know you had nothing to do with what happened and I don't blame you."

"That is very kind of you, Vince. I can't say I blame you for being suspicious after everything that's happened. I sure would be."

"Thanks. Mind if I come over for a few?"

"Not at all, stop on by." She sounded like she was looking forward to it.

†

Even though I had been in Mrs. Arlington's house a million times, somehow it all felt oddly foreign to me then. We sat across from each other in her living room; the squishy, mismatched furniture gathered around haphazardly as usual. I was perched on the red velvet armchair, while Mrs. Arlington was on the beat-up old couch, her hands folded across her lap. I knew she wasn't angry. Every person has one emotion that they do well. Some people just exude joy. I know people who anger suits like a second skin. I've known Mrs. Arlington for years and I have yet to see her angry. I just can't picture it. Sadness is Mrs. Arlington's emotion. When something is bothering her, she doesn›t just get sad, sadness totally envelopes her.

But nothing caused her more sadness than her stepson Morgan. I'd never met the guy, but from what I'd heard he was a colossal fuck up. Mrs. Arlington had been married to Morgan's father and really looked at Morgan like her own child. In fact, she was better to him than his biological mother, a nasty little woman named Joan who could drink like a fish.

My carpet had more maternal instincts than Joan ever did. It was beyond pathetic. Since Morgan had been in and out of rehab and who knows what else, it's safe to say he took after his mother.

Of course, that's not to say Mrs. Arlington was a doormat, not by any stretch of the imagination. She loved Morgan, but she was also tough on him. Not once had I ever heard her make any excuse for him. She would always say, "Right is right and wrong is wrong." I first learned about him about two months after I met her. We were talking about something totally unrelated and she mentioned her stepson. When I asked what he did for a living, she paused for a moment and said he was "going through a rough time." But the look on her face said it all. As time went on, I eventually got the full picture about what he was like.

Once I came home to discover Mrs. Arlington standing in her doorway with a vacant look on her face. Apparently Morgan had tried stealing her identity to score some cash for a quick pick-me-up. When she learned what was going on, she promptly called the police and they arrested Morgan, who was in a bar somewhere about three hours away. That was a year ago and it was the last she heard about him. Since I felt really bad about the situation, I took her out for dinner later that week. We went to Red Lobster, her favorite. But I gotta give her credit, because while we were waiting to order, she added as an afterthought, "I was hoping Morgan would become a different person, but that was just bullshit."

The situation with Morgan was a big reason why I got to know her well. She deserved so much better. Part of me wondered if she knew before who Allison was, would things have been different? I bet she beats herself up about that now, too.

"So, what do you want to talk about?" she eventually asked in the calm, interested tone of a high school guidance counselor. Except she was genuinely interested and didn't care about my ACT score.

"I just wanted to see how you were." Mrs. Arlington smiled at this. A genuine one.

"That's kind of you to ask, I am doing ok. I totally understand why you needed some time to yourself. No one could blame you."

"Thanks." I slowly began telling her what I'd learned in the meantime. Once I was finished, her smile was gone. She looked absolutely stunned.

"My God, I don't even know what to say."

"I know."

"Just know that if you need anything, I will do everything I can to help you."

"Oh yes I know. And I'm sorry about being paranoid."

"Sweetie, I would have been worried about you if you weren't. I told you already, I don't blame you one bit for being suspicious of me. Hell, I sure would be in your shoes. You've been through a lot. I get it."

With that, our conversation went back to how it always was. I made sure to ask about her sister and niece; her sister was doing fine and her niece had made the honor roll in school like she always did. I made sure to give her a big hug before I left. As I went back to my house, I felt better than I had in a while. The next few days were rather uneventful. I kept to my work at the university, but as I always do these days, I kept my eyes and ears open.

†

I was heating up some soup for dinner later that week when I heard the phone ring. According to the caller ID, it was Ramsay.

"Hello?"

"Hey, Vince. Detective Ramsay here. Got an update for you."

"Shoot."

"Well, according to the other bits of footage on the flash drive, Allison had a few other stuffed animals besides the one she took with her to the hospital."

"That's right,"

"They were there on the video you saw, but in subsequent videos we witnessed people not just coming and taking them but putting them back as well."

"That's really weird."

"I know. They didn't take any valuables or anything. You can clearly see some expensive jewelry on her chest of drawers, but they were never touched."

"Do you know who any of the people are?"

"A couple are a few local lowlifes who we are in the midst of tracking down. The others we aren't sure of."

"Why would they care about what random stuff she kept around the house?" The answer hit me before he could say another word

"I think you have an idea, am I right?" I felt cold chills run through my body as he asked.

"Yes. She has a habit of stashing things inside stuffed toys, why would those be any different?"

"Exactly."

"That's also what she wanted people to see isn't it?" I heard myself asking Ramsay. My own voice felt foreign; hollow and lifeless.

"Yes. It makes too much sense. Have you heard of the madman theory?"

"Sounds vaguely familiar."

"Basically, it means that sometimes it is a strategic choice to act insane. At times, insanity is a rational act when it is motivated by logical concerns."

"You think she faked being crazy to get away with murder or something?" I heard Ramsay emit a heavy sigh on the other line. I have no idea if he smoked, but I could imagine him taking a long drag on a cigarette right about now.

"I don't think she faked that, but I do think someone wanted her to seem crazy."

"Why?"

"To hide something or initiate something. The same something I believe is behind the note or two you have received. But obviously they know you aren't in the know. Millstone on the other hand was. Or he knew something."

"Right."

"I have to ask you for a small favor. Do you mind meeting me for dinner and seeing if you recognize anyone we saw in Allison's apartment?"

"Where and when?"

†

Less than an hour later I was walking into Maria's Ristorante, which was about 20 minutes away. All Ramsay had to ask was if I liked Italian and I was off. The heavy wooden door slammed behind me as I crossed the threshold. The place had giant murals of the Italian countryside painted on the walls. At the far end of the main dining room I found Ramsay. I wasted no time in taking the seat opposite him in the booth, the thick violet tablecloth hanging over the edge of the table. Before I knew it, the waitress was hustling over to take our order; I ordered chicken piccata while Ramsay ordered veal parmesan. When she walked away it was just the two of us again.

"Thank you for coming, Vince," he said after taking a sip of water. The ice chinked merrily in the glass as he raised it to mouth. I could see the condensation glistening on it as he set it back down in front of him.

"No problem. I could have just come down to the station if you had questions for me."

"Oh no, I won't subject you to that any more than I absolutely have to. You've earned a decent meal for all that's happened. Your cooperation has been of enormous help to us."

"I just want this over and done with,"

"Totally understand. We all do."

"Mind if I see those pictures now?" He reached into his jacket pocket and handed me a few pieces of paper that had been folded in half. As I took them and began going through each one, I counted six in all. I recognized the various stuffed animals from Allison's place, all things she had acquired over the years; a monkey, a cat, a lion, a red teddy bear, a dog, and a large yellow smiley face were all spread out before me.

"Yup. All hers."

"Any stories behind these specific ones?" Ramsay sat watching me with his arms resting on the edge of the table.

"Apart from the smiley face which I gave her, I can't remember. But I don't think so. If she was sentimental towards any of these, believe me she would have gone on for hours about it," I offered as I handed him back the photos.

"Why did you give it to her? Special occasion?"

"No, we went to a carnival a while back and I won it playing ski-ball. That was the prize and I let her keep it."

"Nice gesture. Thank you, Vince. That's enough of that for now."

He spent the rest of the time asking about me personally instead of Allison. It was a nice change. When they brought us fresh bread and our salads, I took the chance to ask Ramsay about himself. As I dug into my house salad, he told me about his family; married with two daughters.

"A giant handful," he added with a good-natured eye roll.

After they took the empty salad plates away, we chatted about our various interests. When he told me that his favorite movie was *Wall Street*, I couldn't help but be a bit surprised. Part of me was expecting him to say *Lethal Weapon* or something.

"Because that's how crime works. It quietly seduces people by telling them that not only can they have the life they want, but they can get it quicker and better that way," he explained. Ramsay had a solid point there.

"Very true. Not to mention Charlie Sheen looks like a different person entirely."

"That he does."

"I was expecting your favorite movie to be *Die Hard*." He looked up for a moment and immediately started laughing.

"Good one. I do like it, though."

"Me too, I watch it every year after I finish my Christmas shopping."

"Good man. Without a doubt, it's the most accurate portrayal of how much office Christmas parties suck. I mean come on, that party was almost dead before McClane showed up." Now it was my turn to start laughing.

"Sure was."

Our food came shortly after that. Ramsay made sure they loaded a ton of parmesan cheese on top of the spaghetti that came with his veal. It sat there on the plate like a pile of fresh snow. It was real cheese too, not the stuff that looks and tastes like sawdust. I automatically liked him more for that. I don't get people who can eat pasta without parmesan cheese. After we ate, I sat there comfortably full while he was having coffee. Ramsay took his with two sugars and a splash of milk. About halfway through the cup, he brought up the case again. That wasn't surprising, in his line of work people are probably far more open and easier to deal with after they've had a good meal. He placed the porcelain cup back on the matching plate and folded his hands in front of him.

"We double checked the mental institution. According to records that were repeatedly verified, Allison was searched for anything potentially hazardous upon her admittance. That includes going through the bear.»

"So that means she got the stuff while she was there?"

"Correct."

"How?"

"That's what we're working on. Since I've worked with Dr. Burton a few times over the years, I have complete confidence in him. He's a standup guy. I think that is where Millstone comes in."

"He gave it to her?"

"I think so. But what doesn't make sense is that if he wanted her dead, why would he seem so upset over her death?"

"Perhaps she told him she wanted to die."

"Very possible. I'll be dropping by the hospital soon to see if they recognize either the stuff they took from her place or the people who took them. I'll also be taking a look at their security footage, it should make ID'ing people a lot easier. We have a few potential leads, but this could really speed it up."

"Good deal." I got out my wallet to pay for my food, but Ramsay quickly waved it away.

"On me, Vince."

"Thank you." That was far better than the minestrone soup I was planning on having.

"Believe me, the gratitude is all mine. This case is a weird one and you've been extremely helpful. On that note, here are some of the guys we're looking into that were on the footage. Recognize any of them?" I didn't recognize any of them, but one looked familiar somehow. It was a bit like seeing a character actor on TV and thinking you'd seen them before, but couldn't remember what else you saw them in. The guy was in his mid to late 20s, lean but sturdy build, with a shaved head and dull brown eyes. I briefly tapped my finger on his picture.

"He looks kind of familiar, but apart from that, no."

"Appreciate it. Anything you can do to stir up some new information would be helpful. We're keeping an eye on you and your place, so don't worry about safety or anything. We also know about Mrs. Arlington. She came to us voluntarily and told us everything she knows." I felt my usual affection for her.

"She's a terrific lady."

"She is indeed. Way better than Mrs. Dunbar. That woman should've never had children."

"Do you know where she is?"

"Honestly, no. Allison was committed to the psych ward by an aunt who was her primary contact in case of emergencies. She is also who claimed Allison's body. I'm calling some old contacts in the state police and they're seeing what they can dig up."

"Good deal. I'll do what I can as well."

"That's all we ask. The reason I mention it is because while we don't usually ask people to go out and dig on their own, I know that is sort of your job. History and anthropology and whatnot. You've got an impressive resume."

"I appreciate that Detective."

"Just the truth. Quite frankly it's great background for this sort of thing and not all that different from what I do; digging up small details and occasionally finding something morbid. Not to mention, our subject is the same.»

"And that is?"

"The dead and what's already happened. But not really, we're searching for how people lived and what happened when they died. Finding out how someone died is easy. If I say someone died of a heart attack, that's a statement. But if I say someone died of a heart attack because someone deliberately messed with their medication, that's a crime."

"Sure is." Ramsay was onto something. "Most people don't have the slightest idea what anthropology is. The best I usually get is something about *Jurassic Park*. I don't get too upset about that though, because I love the movie."

"But they are onto something about the nature of your work, as well as mine to a larger extent. That movie took the idea of studying what existed long ago to see how it lived to an extreme level. While I certainly don't clone dinosaurs, I encounter a lot of people when they're already dead, but what I really need to know is what happened to them when they were alive."

"Well said, Detective."

"So on that note, don't be shy about digging. Ms. Dunbar didn't have a lot of friends around here. Loner type if I ever saw one." He was really on the money there, Allison went through 'friends' like fads. She might be reciting the life history of some girl named Tiffany one moment, only to inform me within a few weeks that Tiffany was no longer her friend.

"That's for sure."

"The seeds of a crime are usually planted long in advance. It's just that no one realizes anything is growing. So, I would bet those seeds were sown elsewhere. It seems Miss Vale might be able to help with that. In fact, I think she might want to help you out with a few things," he added with a knowing grin.

"What do you mean?" I hastily replied. But I was pretty sure I knew what he meant.

"She's a nice girl. I've checked her out as well; fine record, no issues or anything. I also don't think she would give two shits about what happened to the Dunbar girl if she didn't care about you. If you were an asshole and she didn't like you, would she be out here trying to help solve this and make sure you were ok?"

"Probably not." I waited for Ramsay to say something more about that, but he didn't. That was another little gesture of his I appreciated. After we both declined dessert, Ramsay paid for our food and we left it at that.

✝

After I got home, I started thinking about what Ramsay had said. After turning on the TV, I stared at the bookshelf to the left of the couch as I tried to think of why that guy looked familiar. As I thought of something, a cold wave of dread washed over me.

The most likely reason was because he was once a student at the university. Who knows, maybe he was even in one of my lectures. Teaching at a university will expose you to a ton of kids, most of whom you will only vaguely recognize. Unlike in a grade school or high school, working at a university means that you meet so many students, it's impossible to remember them all. It didn't even have to be someone from a class of mine. Odds are even better it could just be someone I saw on campus. The guy was younger, definitely in his mid-twenties, so he was around the right age. The mere thought of it made me shudder. Believe me, Greenbriar University was a decent place and all, but we had our share of unsavory types. The opioid crisis hit it HARD. Not just students, but at least three of my former colleagues were in rehab trying to beat it. The saddest part is that those are just the ones I know about.

Since Allison had been to see me at work several times herself, odds were good that a scumbag first encountered her there. Believe me, she would have turned plenty of heads on the way to my office. One time she was even down to play the whole "sexy student comes to see her professor" routine. Not gonna lie, I really enjoyed that. It was September 24th, I remember because it was one of her birthday gifts to me. That memory almost seemed like a different era.

†

Ramsay picked up on the third ring.

"Vince, what's up?" I could tell he was trying not to sound concerned or excited.

"I just thought of something. I have an idea of where I might recognize him from."

"Where?"

"Work. I think he may have gone to Greenbriar University or may have even been in one of my lectures."

"Damn, that's good thinking. Odds are you may be right too. I'll get on this immediately. I'll go to the registrar first thing tomorrow and see if I can't find a match."

I hung up the phone and tried to get my mind onto something pleasant. While I wanted Ramsay to find out what happened, I really hoped he wouldn't find him at the place I work.

14

During the next couple days, I looked at everyone at work with suspicion. For every person I encountered the thought, 'Could it be
them?' flashed in my head like some sick guessing game. Even students
and younger members of the staff who I knew relatively well weren't im-
mune to my new sense of paranoia. In fact, they made me even more suspicious than those I barely recognized. How much did they really know
about my life? It brought me right back to the moment when Allison
became a cheater. She had been to the university several times and I had a
picture of us on my desk. They always say a cheater does it with someone
known to the person they're cheating on, so odds are it could have been
someone right there. The idea made me more paranoid than anything
else that had happened thus far. The stuff that happened at home was one
thing. But this was my work, my profession, something I took immense
pride in.

The only thing I can compare it to is something out of *Invasion of
the Body Snatchers*. I didn't know anything for certain, but odds were good
that someone out there was not what they seemed. So, I did what I always
do when I feel uneasy; get down to work and keep a close watch on things.

You might not suspect this, but teaching at a college level is actually quite helpful in dating, because you get plenty of experience seeing
through deception and immaturity. As a result, it helps you screen people. Romantic prospects are a lot like students; the serious ones always

make themselves known. Someone who isn't into you is no different than students who don't bother with the assigned reading. They always have some excuse.

†

Later that week, Ramsay called me in the middle of lunch.

"Hey Vince, got some news for you."

"Ok." I put down the fork I was eating a Caesar Salad with and gripped the phone tighter.

"I don't think that guy is a student. I couldn't find anyone in the registrar's office that matches his description and I went through every photo of students born after 1989. Also checked out the staff. No matches there either." As Ramsay said this, I felt my entire body relax. It was one of those tensions where you're so wound up that you don't even realize it until it passes.

"Well, that's good. I don't think I could stand if it did turn out to be someone from here."

"Don't blame you one bit. It was a solid theory and we knocked out a lot of suspects, so good job. Just keep doing your thing and I'll check back if I have any leads."

I went back to my salad, suddenly feeling much hungrier than before Ramsay called. After I was done with it, I walked out of my office with the mounds of books and papers everywhere and stopped at the vending machine at the far end of the hall. Popping in some change, I punched the button for C5; a two pack of Reeses. I immediately devoured them when I got back to my office. Unsurprisingly, they tasted fantastic. Nothing goes better with good news than dessert.

Before I knew it, the workweek was over and it was time to meet Chloe for our night out. I hadn't been nervous before, but now I was feeling it big time. Dressing in a nice black button up, I chose some respectable cologne; the kind that says, 'I want to smell decent, but not go all formal.' As I was heading out my front door, I couldn't help but think, *What do you have to lose?*

The answer was a resounding nothing. Looking back on all that had happened before this moment, pursuing whatever this was could not possibly be worse than the whole Allison situation. That's the great thing about extreme circumstances. Once they're over, there isn't much that can rattle you. The only way to go is up.

In seemingly no time at all, I was in front of her hotel and she emerged out of the lobby right on schedule.

"Hey there," she greeted me happily. "Ready to go?" She had this lightness about her I hadn't seen before. It was like seeing a totally different person. As she got in the car I noticed she was wearing a crimson colored blouse, tight black jeans, and a tan leather jacket that looked incredibly soft. It was a good look for her. I also caught a faint whiff of vanilla as she closed the door. It was a soothing smell.

"You know it."

We went to a bistro where they had opened the patio for dinner. A gentle breeze glided through the tables, making the trendy lanterns drift lazily in the wind. The balmy spring air gave the entire place a calm, content feeling. As we sat down at our table, I suddenly realized that the nerves from earlier had completely faded away. I hadn't felt this good about a date for a long time. I had been on a couple dates here and there, but having dinner with Chloe somehow just made sense. Like there was none of that first date awkwardness. It was a very nice change of pace. She got penne pasta with vodka sauce, while I ordered a flatbread pizza. Chloe had the waiter put so much parmesan cheese on her food she actually put Ramsay to shame. It reminded me of my parents, who to this day put so much cheese on spaghetti sometimes you can't even see the noodles when they are done.

Sitting there, I totally forgot how we met. We were just like any other couple out for a nice dinner. Now that felt downright amazing. We just chatted away about ordinary things and ate contently.

Before I knew it, darkness had set in and it was almost 11 p.m.

"I really hate to cut this short, but it's getting late and we should probably get back."

"You're right." She stood up from her chair and began to put her coat back on while I left the waiter a healthy tip. We drove back to her hotel quietly and as the clock hit 11:20, I pulled into the hotel parking lot. The moon was popping out of the sky that night, luminescent against the midnight blue sky. The parking lot was also rather quiet that time of night.

"I really had fun tonight. One of the best dates I've been on in a long time," she said gratefully, making no attempt to get out of my car.

"Same here. It really meant a lot to me."

"Do it again soon?'" She asked hopefully, her eyes glimmering faintly against the hotel's illuminated exterior.

"That would be great." Without saying another word, she leaned forward and kissed me. Her lips were inviting, soft and comforting. I gladly returned the gesture for what seemed like a few seconds until she pulled away. As she did, I noticed the slight flush on her cheeks.

"Goodnight, Vince. I'll talk to you in the morning," she practically whispered as she took off her seat belt. "I really enjoyed tonight."

"Me too. Sleep well," I waited until she got back into the hotel before driving off. When I got home I changed clothes and climbed into bed, switching on the TV as I did. I felt happy, better than I had in a very long time. This felt, dare I say it, normal. Before I knew it, I drifted off to reruns of *CSI*.

†

Waking up the next morning, I slept so well that as I opened my eyes, I forgot what day it was. The memory of last night settled back over me as I leaned back on my pillow. I couldn't get over how different Chloe was from most women I'd gone out with in the past. Some women I knew from work could never stop talking. While, believe me, I love a stimulating conversation, there comes a point where it's not so much a conversation as it's a monologue. The flip side of this is the dating equivalent of lecturing for a class that is not paying attention. The person might be physically there, but mentally they are light years away, probably fantasizing about someone else. The funny thing is that sometimes people can go back and forth between those extremes, which usually happens in relationships that aren't going well.

You know why most people see a therapist? It's typically because of their relationships. It may not be due to a romantic one; it could also be because of a parent, child, or sibling. But when you really look at it, a therapist is a lot like a significant other. You slowly reveal parts of yourself to a complete stranger until they see you at your most raw and vulnerable. The only difference is that with a therapist, one is emotionally naked, and with a significant other you get physically naked. But here's a little secret; usually in a serious relationship you slowly but steadily find yourself emotionally exposed as well. Now imagine if your therapist betrayed your trust and didn't respect what intimate details you had shared with them. That's a bad relationship in a nutshell.

But why do we date the people we date? Because something about them appeals to us. The challenge of dating is trying to figure out what exactly it is that you like so much. If a breakup happens, it's because you reach the sad revelation that what appealed to you so much either isn't there anymore, it no longer entices you, or was all an illusion.

I liked Chloe because she was caring, driven, dependable, interesting, and different. Most girls I know would have run like hell from a situation like this. Not her. Plus, it didn't hurt that she was very attractive. I spent the rest of the day in a pleasant mood; classes were about to let out for the summer, so anticipation was in the air. Much as I enjoy work, I love summer because I go traveling and spend about a month with my parents down in Florida. After going for a run outside, I made myself some waffles.

†

Chloe came by around dinnertime the following day. The weather had turned drab and it was a chilly, rainy end to the weekend. I was surprised when I answered the door, because she was carrying a bunch of groceries. While she had given me a heads up she was on her way, I wasn't expecting her to bring food.

"Hey, I thought since we usually go out and stuff I should make sure you get a nice home-cooked meal." I was temporarily speechless.

"I'm not gonna complain about that."

"Good, because I'm a great cook and I'm tired of cooking for just my-self. Not to mention, I'm so over takeout, restaurants, and room service."

She immediately found her way around my kitchen and in no time at all, she was chopping away at some vegetables. I was still a bit stunned. Let me sum up Allison's cooking ability; the idea of eating something she made or even her attempting to cook something in my kitchen terrified me far more than anything that happened after we broke up. Chloe, on the other hand, almost looked more comfortable in there than I was.

"Need any help?" I offered from the doorway.

"Sure," she smiled at me from her spot by the counter. "I'm making lasagna; you can boil the noodles while I get the sauce ready. They're in the bag on the table." I did as she asked and before I knew it, dinner was ready. By then my house smelled inviting and cozy; garlic and cheese hovered in the air. The food tasted amazing and there were a ton of leftovers. Which was just fine with me, because like anything else tomato-based, lasagna is always amazing the second day.

After dinner we settled down to watch *The Big Lebowski*, one of the greatest movies ever created by man. I was even tempted to make a White Russian. Watching the scene with Donny's ashes in the coffee can, I had a sudden thought. What if someone had just tossed Allison into a jar or something? I could totally see some single IQ dumbass scattering her ashes right into the face of some random person.

"Do you think Allison was out of her element and did it all to her-self?" Chloe asked me out of nowhere after the movie was over.

"Why do you ask?"

"Well, the movie made me think of it." I knew what she meant, al-though the movie was far more amusing than the Allison situation. I sat there for a moment while I thought it over.

"She did something to herself. It's just a matter of what." She nodded her head in agreement.

As Chloe reclined back on the couch, I noticed something. I don't know if it was just me noticing after all this time, but Chloe had really nice legs. One might be tempted to call them lovely. She had her jeans rolled up to her knees and was sitting cross-legged beside me, a pillow cushioning her arms. Her legs looked soft and yet incredibly toned, with a nice honey color. Not orange from some cheap spray tan. Slowly, the overwhelming urge to reach out and touch them crept up on me. Maybe it's a guy thing, but a woman's legs can be so underrated. In this day and age, it's easy to forget how way back, a leg was the gold standard of sexy.

Suddenly, she turned to look at me. I felt nervous, almost like she could read my thoughts. I was about to put on a different movie or something when without saying a word, she scooted closer, leaned back and put her legs up on mine. Almost like a reflex, I put a hand on the top part of her right leg. I could feel her relax almost immediately. The ease of it all took me by surprise; it felt like the most routine thing in the world. I felt a small wave of heat surge through my body. Her skin was even softer than I imagined. We sat there a while in comfortable silence, just relaxing.

"I think it's time we paid Millstone's wife a visit," I said eventually. She nodded but didn't say anything at first.

"Whenever you're ready."

"Cool. Dan Millstone was important to Allison; but why?"

"He cared about her for some reason and it seems they got physical."

"Right, but he also had the teddy bear. The one that smuggled the drugs she used to kill herself."

"He died in a fire, right?"

"Correct."

"Usually fire is used to get rid of something."

"Yup. According to the news, the place was damaged pretty badly. Odds are the family had to move out for a spell."

"Think Dr. Burton knows where they can be reached?"

"Only one way to find out."

†

Dr. Burton did indeed know where to find the Millstones. They were living in some development just outside of town. They had moved because of the fire damage to their old house.

"You think they will talk to me?" I asked him.

"I know his wife. She is a terrific lady. Her name is Joanna. I told her if she needs anything to come and talk to me. If you like, I can tell her I'm sending someone to meet her; someone she has something in common with."

"That'd be great. Thanks doctor."

"Oh, and Vince?"

"Yes?"

"The same applies for you. If you need anything at all, you know where to find me."

"Thanks."

15

The next day I picked up Chloe at her hotel for our little meeting with Mrs. Millstone. It was a gorgeous Tuesday; the late afternoon meant the sun was high in the sky, looming over the horizon.

"Hey you," she called to me as she hopped in the passenger seat and I began to peel out of the parking lot. "Do you think Mrs. Millstone knew about Allison?" She continued as I headed towards the highway.

I took a second to answer her, as I had never thought about that before.

Infidelity is a lot like murder, because the people involved are typically familiar with each other beforehand. Infidelity tends to linger, slowly growing in silence with every encounter. But it doesn't grow like a normal plant. Dangerous thoughts like those grow like a weed. Infidelity is the nasty little dandelion that once planted, is almost impossible to eradicate. All it takes is for one act of infidelity to fully bloom and that seed is forever planted in the mind.

"Perhaps." That was the best answer I could give. Mrs. Millstone herself might not know what she knows.

As we drove on, I thought about her husband's obituary. I wonder how closely it reflected the real person. An obituary is like making a Tinder profile, or any other social media account. It's an attempt to present an individual in the best possible light that usually does nothing to capture the essence of the real person. For every dating profile or obituary, there is someone who can claim that every word of it is fiction. But I'd definitely have to say obituaries were the more honest of the two. Just look at the 40-year-old soccer mom trying to hide that she isn't in her twenties anymore. On Tinder, you might be able to hide that. But the best selfie lighting imaginable is useless for an obituary.

"Did you ever see Allison's obituary?" I asked, shooting Chloe a brief look as I passed a red SUV with a 'Proud Parent of an Honor Student' bumper sticker slapped on the back of it.

"Yeah, I did. Nothing much in there really. She was born, she died, she will be dearly missed. Loving daughter and good friend."

"How original."

"I know. Totally sums her up right?" Chloe rolled her eyes as she took a sip of the bottled water she brought with her.

"Millstone had one advantage that most of us guys don't have. He at least knew the girl was crazy before he went for it. They don't have that shit on Tinder."

"I suppose that is a perk."

"They need to make an app for that. It'd be worth a fortune in no time."

"Definitely."

"Can I make a bad joke?"

"Absolutely."

"Millstone had the ultimate Tinder profile. Just ask the fire department." Chloe looked at me for a second before lightly hitting my shoulder.

"You're terrible," she added, laughing in spite of herself.

"You know it's funny." I was proud of that one. Gotta find the humor amidst the insanity. We cruised along the road, getting off on Exit 27. I followed the newly laid blacktop winding along before us. It looked so fresh I could practically smell the earthy, slightly singed smell of fresh tar.

The Millstones lived in one of those moderately big development houses. The kind that screamed well off orthodontist or accountant. After a short turn around the cul-de-sac, we parked in front of a grey brick house with a tiny, but neat yard. I wasn't sure what I expected Mrs. Millstone to look like, but for some reason I kept imagining a wispy woman with mousy hair. The woman who answered the door was anything but; she was tall, with an athletic figure, lush auburn hair, and catlike green eyes.

"Joanna Millstone?" She stood up straighter at the mention of her name.

"Yes?"

"Dr. Burton mentioned I might be visiting. I'm Vince O'Malley and this is Chloe. We're here to talk about your husband." At the mere mention of Dr. Burton's name, she instantly stood up straighter.

"Please come in." She quickly stepped aside and gestured that we should come inside. Our shoes thudded silently on the plush brown welcome mat laid out inside the front hallway. "Right this way," she continued as she led us to the kitchen area. "Can I offer you two a drink? Water, tea, coffee?"

"No thank you," I said.

"I'm fine too. But thanks for offering," Chloe added.

"No problem. Make yourselves comfortable." She pointed to the sitting room just past the dining room. I noticed that the TV room downstairs was messy with toys; Legos and action figures mostly. The house didn't have much furniture, but since they had a nasty fire and were forced to move, that didn't surprise me. We sat down on a navy-blue sofa while Mrs. Millstone sat across from us in the matching recliner.

"Thank you for seeing us, Mrs. Millstone," I began after Chloe and I sat down on the couch. She crossed her right leg over her left as she took a sip of coffee.

"Oh, it's no problem. Dr. Burton is a standup guy."

"That he is. First of all, we would like to say how sorry we are for your loss." Mrs. Millstone nodded in understanding.

"I appreciate that very much."

"I'm not really sure how to say this, but here goes." I felt my mouth take on the consistency of cotton as I prepared to continue. "When your husband passed away and they posted the obituary, I saw the picture of your family. I've seen the teddy bear your daughter was holding before."

"Where?" she looked surprised, but not entirely shocked.

"A girl I used to date was carrying it around right before she was placed in the institution where your husband worked. That's how I know Dr. Burton."

"You're not serious," she whispered faintly.

"I'm afraid so. That's not even the worst part. The girl killed herself in the hospital. Using drugs that she had concealed inside that thing." I had no idea how she would react. Maybe she'd get angry or tell us we were wrong. But she just sat there.

"Daniel and the girl." It came out as more of a statement than a question.

"I'm so sorry Mrs. Millstone."

"Don't be. I wish I could say I was surprised. He'd been acting odd for a little while before his death. Hell, his death itself was odd. Unfortunately, that didn't surprise me either."

"Why?" Chloe asked before I could.

"There were many parts to my husband. Some were better than others. Most importantly, he was a good father. Whatever else I can say about him, that is the most important. Daniel also loved his work as a paramedic. Told me he loved the rush, the thrill of it all. You see, he loved to gamble. The type of bet never mattered. I always thought work was an extension of that for him. Trying to beat the odds and all that nonsense."

"I see."

"But you know how this story goes. He couldn't stop and owed money to people you don't want to owe money to. The kind of people who always get their investment back; the house that always wins, one way or another."

"Right,"

"That was my first thought when I heard about the fire. Insurance money and all that. Sadly, I wish that was all it was. I knew he had gambling issues, but I didn't know the depths that he went to in order to straighten things out. Daniel didn't have money, but he had access. Access to addicts, drugs, and other stuff that fetches a pretty penny."

"He was a middleman?" I asked, shifting slightly on the couch while paying close attention to what she was saying.

"I'm not sure what to call it exactly, but that probably isn't a bad way to put it. Most of the time, they used him when they didn't want to have to bring someone to the ER. Off the books type stuff. Someone gets shot in a deal gone bad and you can't have any questions asked, who better to call than the medic who owes you one? I honestly don't know that much myself. Whenever they needed him for a special job, they'd call on a special phone they gave him. A burner."

"He spoke several languages, right?" She nodded briefly.

"Yes. It was quite handy for patients who didn't speak English or didn't speak it well."

"Thanks again for talking with us about this," Chloe added from beside me.

"It's quite alright," Mrs. Millstone replied nonchalantly before taking another sip of coffee. «Daniel is gone and from what you said Vince, it seems we have something in common.» She raised her hands in a ‹eh, what can you do?› gesture.

"I suppose we do. Did anyone else know about your husband bringing home the bear? Did you post any pictures of your family like the obituary picture?"

"Let me think," Mrs. Millstone looked upwards as if hoping the answer would fall from the sky. "I probably did. As you can imagine, my dear husband didn't exactly tell me where he got the bear. I guess he was keeping that little bit of information all to himself." She spat the last word out, making the final syllable sounding almost like a hiss. I felt truly horrible for her.

"Indeed. Well, you aren't the only one to get an unpleasant surprise in a toy. Someone left a doll version of me at my house months ago, while I also recently discovered that the girl the bear originally belonged to hid video footage inside said doll. The footage was of her screwing and killing some guy." Mrs. Millstone sat there for a few moments, her face the blank mask of someone who doesn't know quite what to say.

"I can't believe I'm saying this, but you actually beat me in the fucked-up story department," she finished sympathetically.

"I beat most people these days. But what happened to the bear?"

"It's still here." Her voice dropped to a whisper, so I almost couldn't hear her, "Do you think?"

"Only one way to find out." At this point, my voice was barely louder than hers. She immediately walked out of the room and I heard her hustle up the stairs. Moments later, Mrs. Millstone was rushing back with that thing. She held it extended away from her with two fingers, as if she was afraid it was contaminated by some horrible disease. Maybe it was. Just looking at it was unpleasant enough.

"Open it," I heard Chloe suggest, her voice also a hushed whisper.

Mrs. Millstone opened the back of the stuffed bear and looked inside, like she was digging through her purse. She also tipped it over and shook it hard. I don't know what I was expecting or hoping for, but nothing happened. I then realized that both Chloe and I had stood up and moved closer to the bear.

"Well, that's that," Mrs. Millstone said after a minute. "I can't find anything. I don't know if that's good or bad."

"It's new information we have, which is good," Chloe said encouragingly. "Mind if we take it with us?"

"Be my guest. I never want to see this again." She immediately thrust the bear at Chloe, who put it carefully by her feet as we resumed our seats.

"Do you have any idea if Allison knew your husband had gambling debts?" I asked, my voice returning to normal.

"While I can't say for certain, if she had ties to shady people around town, it's certainly possible. Especially when you add in the fact he knew about that stuffed thing.

"That makes sense,"

"But I know he would never deliberately or knowingly harm her. Daniel became a paramedic because he loved helping people. Part of that stemmed from our daughter."

"Your daughter?" Chloe asked, her hands clasped in front of her.

"Yes. Our very first child together died shortly after birth. A stillborn; Sophie was her name. I took it very hard, but Daniel took it even worse. I have never seen a human being so totally destroyed by grief in my life."

"I'm so sorry, Mrs. Millstone." I didn't think it was possible, but somehow, I felt even more sympathy for her.

"Joanna please," she took a deep swig of coffee before continuing. "But we endured. The first year after was absolute agony. I thought things might never get better. But they did. Daniel also decided to become a paramedic around that time. I never asked him, and he never said it out loud, but I always thought that deep down, he wanted to prevent that from ever happening to someone else. So, while I can't say if he ever had a relationship with that girl, I can be sure he never harmed someone else's daughter."

There haven't been many times when I felt a total loss of words, but this was one of them. But that was perfectly fine, as respectful silence seemed totally appropriate. Mrs. Millstone eventually took a deep breath and returned to the subject of our visit.

"I hope this all helps, I really can't think of anything else. Unless there is something else you want to know?" She asked while running a hand through her hair.

"No, that›s all I can think of Joanna. Thank you so much for everything," I finished gratefully as we stood up to leave. Since Chloe was ahead of me, I could see she was carrying the stuffed bear in her right hand. Mrs. Millstone stood up and led us to the same door we came in through. But just before I was about to step outside, she surprised me with a hug.

"Good luck and be careful Vince," she whispered gently to me.

"Thank you."

With that final farewell, I stepped onto the front porch and headed back to my car. As we pulled out of the cul-de-sac, she gave us a friendly wave from her front door.

"Tough woman," Chloe observed as I pulled out of the development. I noticed she had put the bear in my backseat. I couldn't wait to get it out of my sight once and for all. I absolutely hated that thing was in my car. Turning the radio back on, we listened to some classic rock. As I got on the highway, I glanced over I saw she was grooving in her seat and mouthing along to the lyrics, so I turned it up slightly. Somehow, I had the feeling she sang in the shower as well.

†

Ramsay was thrilled when I updated him on what we had just heard. To my immense relief, he was also happy to take the bear off my hands. After dropping Chloe off, I went straight home where Ramsay had agreed to meet me. But before leaving, Chloe gave me a brief kiss on the cheek. As

I was turning onto my street, I could still feel the spot on my cheek that her lips had touched.

"Thanks Vince, I really appreciate this," he greeted me as I was giving him the ratty old thing. "We can now examine it for stuff they may have missed the first time."

"I'm just happy to get this goddamn thing out of my sight."

"I gotcha," he nodded sympathetically. "I wouldn't want this thing around me either if I wasn't a cop."

"Right, well there you have it Detective. That and the info I got is the latest stuff I know."

"Great work Vince. I'll update you when I have any news." As Ramsay went back to his car, I really hoped that this was the last time I ever had to lay eyes on that thing.

After Ramsay left I tossed together a sandwich and parked myself in front of the TV. At this point I had no idea what to expect. I also still wasn't sure why that one guy looked so familiar to me. Who was it? Someone who saw Allison and me when we were together and got jealous? That wasn't too far out of the realm of possibility, as we always had gawkers looking at us every time we went out in public.

Let me rephrase that; SHE got the looks, I got the third degree. Guys would approach her even when we were being openly affectionate with each other. Allison turned them all down, but I never forgot how invisible I felt. Random men would offer to buy her drinks or give her their number like it was nothing. To add insult to injury, guys would look at me as if they could not believe we were together. The worst part of it all was that I didn't blame them.

That must be why that guy looked familiar. One of the many, and I do mean many guys that hit on Allison when I was around. That also explained why I didn't like him even though I wasn't sure who he was. Content with this, I went back to focusing on my turkey sandwich, pausing here and there to include a potato chip. As I studied a particularly misshapen one, I felt relief as I remembered that the spring semester would be officially over tomorrow. I had the final grades ready to go and all that remained was to turn them into the dean's office. Never having to give up that euphoric sense of school being out for summer was definitely one of the best parts of my job.

16

After doing my usual end-of-semester business, I celebrated the end of another school year with Chloe. It was a stunning spring day, warm with a light breeze, perfect for grabbing some frozen yogurt. I loaded mine with hot fudge, caramel, and crushed up Oreos. Chloe wasn't messing around either, because she loaded hers with plenty of peanut butter cups, chopped nuts, hot fudge, and sour gummy worms. We ate while walking along a sidewalk about 10 minutes away from school, taking great care not to make a mess of ourselves. As I reached the middle of the bowl, I asked her something that had been on my mind while wrapping things up earlier.

"Now that Millstone is dead, who else can we talk to that knew Allison? Someone who knew her and her family like you did?" Chloe had her spoon raised to her lips when I spoke. She chewed thoughtfully for a moment before answering.

"Let's see. There's no one around here, so that means someone from our old town or elsewhere. As far as I know, she had no family left there, so that leaves someone from school." She began counting on her fingers as she ticked off people. "Mr. Delany died years ago, Ms. Robinson moved to California before Allison and her family left town, and last I heard Mrs. Edwards has Alzheimer's. So that just leaves Mrs. Hanson. She was an institution at Andrew Jackson. That was our old school," she added, noticing the confused look on my face.

"You think she knew why they left town?"

"Mrs. Dunbar couldn't just yank Allison out of school without saying something. Truancy and all that. Besides, she was too much of a stickler for appearances to let it seem like they just went away without a good reason."

"Fair point. I'm guessing you want us to take a field trip?" She nodded before throwing her now empty Styrofoam container into the nearest garbage can.

"If you don't want to, I totally understand," she began slowly. "No one could blame you for not wanting to bother."

"You know something? I don't mind. Not anymore. I could use a little vacation. It's all sort of therapeutic really."

"Cool. Shall we leave Monday?"

"Sounds good."

†

Sunday afternoon was here before I knew it and that meant packing my suitcase. Preparing for a trip is one thing I really take seriously because a poorly planned trip can spell disaster. I can't tell you how many spring break horror stories I've heard over the years. Attempted kidnapping, robbery, you name it. So that means in addition to bringing all the essentials, I also make sure to leave word of where I'm going. In this case, that meant calling Ramsay. I also couldn't help but be intrigued to see Chloe in a new setting. If you ever really want to get to know someone, take a road trip with them. Being alone in a car for hours on end tends to make people show their true selves. After I had put the last of my clothes away, I called up Ramsay.

"Hey Vince, what's up?" he answered in a nonchalant tone.

"Hey Detective. Just wanted to give you a heads up, Chloe and I are visiting Allison's old hometown. She knows someone who may be able to give us more info on Allison's family."

"Wonderful! I also have some good news for you as well. We were able to obtain some DNA from the bear. It doesn't match Allison's or Millstone's, so it's taking some time to eliminate people. But it's a solid lead. Mind if I meet you two so I can get a sample of your DNA and eliminate your profiles as well?"

"Sure thing. We're planning to leave tomorrow. She's coming by at 9 am, so if you get here before then you can see us before we leave."

"Sounds good, see you then."

†

Ramsay arrived at 8:45 the next morning. After swabbing the inside of my mouth, he put the swab safely inside some special kit he brought along. He was just sealing it up when Chloe arrived. Since I texted her beforehand, she was expecting Ramsay's request and was happy to cooperate. Ramsay was crisply efficient with her as well and several minutes later he thanked us both and was on his way. Then it was our turn to hit the road. As Chloe was putting her bags in the car, I stopped by Mrs. Arlington's to let her know where I was going. Since she had already been my savior once when I wasn't home, there was no way I was leaving the state without telling her. When I did, she immediately pulled me into a hug. I couldn't see her face, but I could practically feel her concern as she whispered, "Be very careful." With that, it was time to hit the road.

The drive passed in relative quiet. We made benign chit chat here and there, but eventually silence would prevail each time. The radio would occasionally require some channel surfing, as it would periodically go to static as various stations passed in and out of frequency. I drove briskly, but without gunning the engine, deftly weaving past the odd slow driver or wide load carrying semi. We occasionally passed the odd car off to the side of the road, its hood up while someone was tinkering under the hood or sitting in the front seat with their ear to a phone. But it was mostly just miles of plain forest, the outskirts dotted with billboards warning us about the dangers of drug abuse, signs for McDonald's, and massive water towers that dotted grass and farms like giant blue obelisks. Here and there, a road would be cordoned off or restricted for maintenance.

†

As the sun burned brightly in the now early afternoon sky, we stopped at the turnpike and got some Subway. I wasn't in the mood for Burger King, Popeye's, or Chipotle. By now I had been driving for over three hours and my breakfast of scrambled eggs now seemed like a long time ago. Getting out of the car to stretch my legs felt amazing. I also felt much more alert after scarfing down my turkey sub. Chloe also wasted no time in chowing down on her roast beef sandwich. After we got back on the road, we drove for about two more hours before we came to an outlet mall. We had been making good time and since you always want to stretch your legs, we strolled around for a bit while doing some window shopping. The mall consisted of a few big-name stores, but it was mostly a collection of bargain joints peddling plastic animal figurines, cheap Native American dreamcatchers, racks of sunglasses, and bargain bin CDs. I could almost hear the top 40 hits playing on the speakers inside as I walked by. While I didn't know exactly how far we had to go, I could almost feel we were getting closer to Allison's old hometown. As we crept towards the state border, I could tell the humidity was getting denser. The air seemed to thicken with each passing mile.

Soon after this, our arrival to Missouri was announced by the famous Gateway Arch appearing out of the horizon amidst the dense blue sky. We had one short visit to make before arriving in Maple Bluffs. My car wove its way through the countless highways, ramps, intersections, and divides before we arrived in Poplar Groves; the posh suburb where Chloe's mother lived. As the sun reached its zenith in the sky, I pulled in front of a row of elegant white brick townhouses and cut the engine.

"It's that one over there," Chloe pointed at one residence with a neat thistle wreath on the black door. "I texted her a few minutes ago and said we were almost here."

"That's good."

The humidity greeted me like a wave as I stepped out of the car. Following Chloe to her mother's front door, I stood behind her on the porch. The townhouse was nice-looking from what I could see; expansive windows neatly covered with white drapes and elegant wrought iron lights stood on either side of the front door, which contained a heavy bronze knocker. But Chloe chose to ring the elegant sounding doorbell instead. Moments later, the door was swiftly opened by a slender woman with immaculate silver hair who wasted no time in hugging Chloe.

"Hello sweetie," I heard her murmur into Chloe's ear.

"Good to see you, Mom."

"Likewise, come on in you two, it's much cooler indoors." Chloe's mother straightened up before heading back inside.

We followed her indoors where the air conditioning hit me almost as intensely as the humidity outside. It was like walking into a department store in the middle of summer. Chloe stood aside to let me pass and she shut the door behind me. I glimpsed a massive watercolor of a pond hanging over the antique bench in the entryway before I got a good look at Chloe's mother. A tall woman with porcelain skin and an immaculate head of long white hair, she was outfitted in a crisp white blouse with a dark purple blazer that matched her slacks and heels. I could imagine her as the high-powered editor of some fashion magazine. Mrs. Vale had also aged very well and had the look of someone who'd taken good care of herself.

"Mom, this is Vince. Vince, this is my mother."

"Mrs. Vale, nice to meet you ma'am."

"Melanie, please." Her handshake with a mixture of poise and strength. The kind that said, "I'm a lady, but don't you dare mistake me for some pushover."

"Of course."

We followed her down to the sitting room where it was just as cool as the rest of the house. The furniture looked expensive, but not so fancy that you didn't dare sit on it. I took a seat on a soft black leather sofa, while Chloe took the matching armchair beside it. Melanie picked up a glass of what looked like lemonade before resuming what I assumed was her usual seat. After politely offering us drinks, she crossed one leg over the other and leaned back in her chair.

"It's lovely to meet you, Vince. I am also sorry to hear about what happened to you."

"Thank you, I appreciate that."

"But I'm not surprised. Not one bit. Poor girl was almost guaranteed a rough life."

"What do you mean?"

"Well, by now you know all about her home situation. Or a fragment of it."

"I know some of it, yes."

"As do I. It still haunts me to this day."

"Why, Mom?" Melanie Vale's entire demeanor had shifted. For a second, I could imagine her not as the elegant woman sitting here, but as she may have looked years ago when she was Allison's neighbor.

"Ever since you told me about what happened I can't stop trying to reconcile the young girl I knew with the woman she became. We're all people, just as we were all once children. Charles Manson was a child once, as was Hitler. A child eventually becomes an adult, but children and adults can both turn into monsters. Before someone becomes infamous, there is a life that came before it. I have always wondered what Allison Dunbar was like as a child. It's a parent thing."

"Right, I can understand that," I added.

"Chloe told me you are a professor. So I'd imagine it would be like if one of your students turned out to be a serial killer. You would see them not only as the criminal, but as the individual from your classes."

"I suppose I would." That was a scenario I hoped to never have to think about. The idea of my ex-girlfriend killing a guy out of what appeared to be self-defense was bad enough.

"On the other hand, I have always had a hard time imagining Claire Dunbar as a child. Something about her makes it hard to envision. The closest I can imagine is that eerily self-aware child who is both gifted and terrifying."

"You didn't like her, I take it?" Melanie Vale chuckled faintly at this.

"That's an understatement. No one, and I mean NO ONE, liked her. Sure, people in our old town respected her, and they most definitely feared her, but no one actually liked her. See the difference?" I nodded in understanding. "You can inspire fear, respect, and genuine affection, but not all three. I'll let you guess which one Claire preferred."

"The same one her daughter preferred."

"Good man. The Dunbar family operated out of fear. That applied as much to outsiders as it did to each other. You could tell when they were out together that it was like a carefully choreographed production, and God help you if you made a mistake."

"Were they always like that?"

"I can't say for certain, but I would bet they were." Melanie took a swig of her drink before placing it back on the coaster set on the mahogany table nearby. "She didn't hold a gun to people's heads or anything, but she had this way about her that you knew not to mess with her. But that wasn't what worried me the most."

"What was that?" I asked, eager to hear what she had to say.

"Chloe, how many times did Allison come to our house?"

"All the time, too many to count."

"Right. Now how many times did you go over there?" Chloe looked down in concentration.

"Ummmmm, not a lot."

"Always seemed like she was finding some excuse to come over and never wanted to go home right?"

"Now that you mention it, yeah." Chloe's eyes widened as her mother continued.

"Allison never said point blank that she was having issues at home, but a couple times I wondered if she wanted to tell me something. Another part of being a parent is that you can practically feel when a kid has something on their mind. But that wasn't the most concerning thing I witnessed."

"What was that?"

"You remember when I had surgery on my knee?" Melanie asked Chloe.

"Yeah Mom, why?"

"When Chloe was in school, I had some surgery on my knee and was laid up for a while," Melanie clarified to me. "To help the pain, they prescribed me a few things, Vicodin mostly. The surgery and the recovery went just fine, but a couple of weeks later Allison was at our house for dinner. While Chloe was downstairs watching a movie, Allison came upstairs and went in the bathroom. Since I was lying down on the living room couch reading a book, she didn't see me. At first, I thought nothing of it. But when I heard her going through drawers and the medicine cabinet, that got my attention. Without saying a word, I walked towards the bathroom and crept up on her. Peering through the faint opening in the door that she left ajar, I asked Allison if she needed something and she about jumped out of her skin. She then began to stammer something incoherent like all kids do when a parent catches them. But since she was holding the orange pill bottle containing some of my leftover Vicodin, I quite literally caught her red handed. When I commented on it, Allison immediately broke down and begged me not to tell her mother. According to her story, Allison had been fooling around with some guy and when one thing led to another, she ended up falling somehow and injuring herself. She was too embarrassed to go to her mother and since she knew I had some painkillers and was doing better, the solution was obvious to her. Allison promised up and down that she would never take so much as a Tylenol from us again without my express permission. Even though I didn't believe her story for a minute, I told Allison that I wouldn't say anything. But if I even suspected she was doing something like that again, it would be the last time she would set foot in my house or speak to my daughter."

"You didn't believe her, Mom?"

"Of course not. I believe she didn't want to talk to her mother about sex, but believe me, unless some guy deliberately beat her or something there is no way she could have injured herself that badly to need prescription painkillers. But since she was your friend as well as our neighbor and I know how hard it can be to fit in, especially in a place like Maple Bluffs, I decided to give her one more chance. But believe me, I kept a close eye on her after that. One thing I noticed when I really paid attention was how she was borderline neurotic about her health. You remember how she was always trying new vitamins or on some fancy health kick that she heard of in some magazine?" Chloe laughed at this.

"Oh my God, I totally forgot. They were usually pretty disgusting too."

I couldn't resist a chuckle at this myself. Chloe's mother was right; Allison was a certifiable hypochondriac. Every little cough or headache was immediately blown up into pneumonia or some new deadly disease she heard about on the news. One time I decided to have a little fun with it. After printing out the symptoms of an illness she couldn't possibly have, I told her there was some new disease the CDC was warning us to be on the lookout for. Then I went down the list of symptoms, asking her if she had any of them. As I did, her eyes widened in horror as she realized that she must have it. With Allison now in full blown panic mode, I handed her the list describing the symptoms of testicular cancer. She stared at it in disbelief for a moment before rolling her eyes, while I laughed my ass off in the kitchen.

"But that's when I knew beyond a doubt that Allison had some issues," Melanie finished solemnly. "Taking meds from someone else's medicine cabinet is a red flag for having a problem. I'm sorry I didn't tell you sooner sweetie," she added before turning to her daughter with a forlorn face.

"Hey, I get it, Mom. You don't exactly tell your kids something like that. Besides, back then no one gave a thought to locking up your medicine cabinet and stuff. You were way ahead of the curve on that."

"I appreciate that sweetie. You remember Mrs. Walsh?" Chloe nodded. "She was a friend of mine," Melanie added for my information. "Remember how she went away on a 'holiday' for a while?"

"Yeah." Chloe replied hesitantly.

"The holiday was a trip to Betty Ford to beat a painkiller addiction. She said it was hell, but it did the trick."

"You know what, that doesn't exactly surprise me."

"I didn't think it would, honey, you're very observant."

"My cousin once had to go for treatment himself," I offered. "If I remember correctly, Arizona was where they sent him."

"Drugs?" Melanie asked.

"That's right," I remembered with a sigh. "It was right before I moved out to teach at the university. Greg is a few years younger than I am and had been acting weird for some time. One night, my aunt found him passed out in his own bodily fluids. Cocaine is a hell of a drug indeed. Or as I prefer to say, cocaine is just hell." A wide smile crept across Melanie's lips at this.

"I like him already," she said, clearly pleased.

"Thank you, that's very kind of you, Melanie."

"Of course. So now you both know the story I wanted to tell you. I also just wanted to see Chloe and meet you Vince, especially because

Chloe talks about you often." At the mention of this, Chloe cleared her throat and began shifting in her seat.

"We appreciate the info Mom, but if that's all, we really should be heading out now."

"I understand sweetie, thank you both for stopping in to see me," she stood up, neatly straightening her slacks before giving her daughter a hug. As she walked over to me, I reached out to shake her hand as she swept me up in a surprisingly tight hug for such a slender woman. "You've definitely earned a goodbye hug, Vince," she offered.

"Thank you very much. It was nice meeting you," I spoke into her shoulder as the elegant white hair bristled my ear. "I'll take good care of her," I added before she let go of me. Melanie smiled widely at this, her magenta lipstick stretching across her face.

"Funny enough, I've never worried about that for a minute. You two be safe and call me if you need anything."

With that, we headed back outside where the wall of humidity was waiting for us.

†

"I'm assuming that's not one of the more pleasant conversations you've had with your mother?" I asked after we were back on the highway.

"Actually, that was a pretty mild one compared to others."

"Were you shocked she didn't tell you that story until now?"

"Not really. Mom learned early on how to be able to keep a secret. That's one thing you learn from living with an alcoholic. You also learn about the different kinds of lies."

"What are those?"

"There are lies you tell strangers, lies you tell people close to you, and last but not least, lies you tell yourself. The last ones are especially brutal."

"That they are." We cruised along and now the St. Louis Arch was looming right in front of us.

"Beautiful isn't it?" Chloe added when she saw me looking at it, her hair blowing on account of her open window.

"Sure is."

"Even though I've lived here for years, I never tire of seeing it."

"I didn't know you lived here."

"Yup," she began before taking off her sunglasses to look at me. "Live and work when I need to. I have a seat on the board of our family business. Nothing major, but I get a vote during the annual meetings."

"Look at you. Don't tell me you have a posh office filled with flowers and a million assistants too."

"Nice fantasy," she snickered before putting her sunglasses back on. "But I have one secretary/assistant who works for the business itself and my office is an ok one with a glass desk. Since my uncle is the one in charge of the actual business, I manage our philanthropic efforts. It's definitely way more rewarding for me personally. I get to feel like I'm actually doing something to make someone's life better you know?"

"I do. What did you specialize in? And please don't say substance abuse."

"Actually, I tended to focus more on mental illness. But one thing I've learned through all this is that one usually comes with the other."

After that, we lapsed into a comfortable silence and drove on until the arch was behind us. But just before we were out of city limits, I realized something. I had probably seen it a million times before, but this was the first time that the Gateway Arch's meaning really hit home for me. It was made to commemorate the journey of those who braved a perilous journey into a strange land. Despite the intense humidity, the eerie similarity still managed to give me a chill.

17

After we passed through St. Louis, the countdown to Maple Bluffs began. First 20 miles, then 15, and from there it went steadily down to single digits. Before I knew it, the sign welcoming us to the city of Maple Bluffs was in front of us, the name written in elegant cursive with the M and B woven together on the thick black and blue sign. Apart from that, it was all a bit anti-climactic, with Chloe only offering a nonchalant, "We're here."

Maneuvering through the city streets, the first thing that came to mind was that the town suited Allison perfectly. When you first saw it, the town looked quite nice; lots of quaint looking Victorian houses with neat front yards.

But as you went in deeper, you began to question your first impression as other images of the town emerged. Like its very name suggested, the town's façade was a bluff. It was just a matter of who bought it. I spotted a closed down Ponderosa Steakhouse and Kmart next to the remnants of what looked like a strip mall. Main street was neat enough with small, but respectable looking business and offices decorating the road. The place also had wonderful water views and the occasional nice house decorating the landscape. But apart from that, it was mostly a cluster of beat-up single-story ranch houses that were a throwback to the early 80's. I could imagine the locals sitting in bars with flickering neon signs repeating the refrain of, «It didn›t used to be like this.»

Of course it didn't. Had it always been like that, no family in their right mind would have ever set up roots here. Places that begin as shitholes and remain shitholes are always reduced to rubble; no survivors, no memories.

The center of town was main street, neatly buffeted by a several brick buildings. Capehart Insurance and a mom and pop restaurant named Josie's stood next to the Maple Bluff City Hall, a looming white building with massive windows that seemed to be peering out over the entire town. It's presence seemed oddly out of place. The other thing I kept noticing was that amongst the fast food joints and remnants of retail were signs advertising something called Hilliard Lake. As we had gotten closer to town, signs had also been advertising it on the highway.

"What happened?" I asked Chloe as we turned onto Spruce Drive.

"To what?" She shifted in her seat to look at me, the seatbelt clicking as she did.

"The town. Every town has a story." She briefly took a sip of her water bottle before answering, the cheap, flimsy plastic crunching in her hand.

"Well, it was sort of a handful of things. For starters, the people in charge of the city itself ran it into the ground. We didn't have one awful mayor, we had several. Of course, back then people didn't know that. Times were great decades ago, everyone was happy. Maple Bluffs wasn't wiped out overnight. It was death by a thousand cuts or an infection that silently spreads everywhere."

"Right. Corruption, incompetence, or both?" On my left was an old junkyard complete with a body shop, the name on the sign illegible from being weathered down. There was an assortment of car parts in a small pile next to an old vending machine.

"Both. Oh and don't forget arrogance. Can't leave out the last member of the unholy trinity."

"Course not."

"People lived high on the hog for so long it was a shock when the butcher's bill arrived. Hell, I can't even remember what the little vanity projects were, but I know some people in town still can. In other words, what comes up, must come down. And down it came indeed. Hard. Now as you can imagine, when a town that was doing so well is suddenly in the red, people naturally want to know why. It's like a dam breaking. It seems to happen overnight, but when you look back, the structure was doomed for years. It's just a matter of who can pick up on it."

"What else?" As Chloe was talking, a *Burger King* sign went past her shoulder. I caught a whiff of the food chain as we went on, the heavy charbroiled smell was alluring.

"That was the same time local industries started to fail," she continued. "This big statewide development corporation diverted river traffic away from local ports and before you even realize it, local business is drying up. The haves all come out ok, but then the have-less and have-not families begin to really feel the pinch. But there is money, it's just a question of what you're willing to do for it."

Money, like misery, loves company and doesn't do well alone. Maple Bluffs was the kind of place that kissed up to the few rich people left in town, all in the hopes that they and their money would stay put. Of course, that doesn't mean people in town like having to suck up to the haves. In fact, odds are they absolutely hate having to play a game of limbo of who can bow lowest before the town bigwigs. Something tells me the Dunbar family got a front row seat to that little charade.

"So that's where Allison got her entrepreneurial spirit from," I eventually added.

"Perhaps. The worst part of all is the few families with money left all love to point at the town and say, ‹Isn›t it awful?› when in reality they absolutely love it. Not only is stuff cheaper, it tightens their grip on local matters. Less competition for stuff."

"That's tragic, but makes perfect sense."

"And around here, you know exactly who you can blame for the town's misfortunes and where to find them. You know where they shop, where their kids go to school, and where their wife gets their hair done."

"I'd imagine so. This strikes me as the kind of place where people remember exactly who didn't tip their daughter when they were waiting tables, but also noticed that the same person also managed to afford an expensive trip to Florida."

"That's right. My family did ok here, but we were one of a very small handful. We also moved away not too long after Allison's family did."

"Good to be back?" I asked nonchalantly.

"Ask me later," she replied with a slight grimace.

"Sure thing, and I forgot to ask. What's Hilliard Lake?"

"Local amusement park. One of the few nice things from the old days that's survived this long."

"Even a shithole town always has one redeeming thing left in it. Fun place?"

"Not bad. The indoor waterpark is pretty cool actually."

"Nice."

†

We eventually stopped at our hotel that was located just outside of town and right near the highway. After getting advice from Chloe on where to stay, I made reservations at the local Best Western before we left home. Traveling as I do for work, I've learned where to stay. You can usually tell what kind of hotel a place is by the title. Motel usually means that there should be a sign out front that says "25 days without a murder." Calling a place an inn is usually a good sign that the place is a bed and breakfast with horrible décor and run by people with no clue whatsoever about how to run a B&B. Now, if it has "suites" anywhere in the title, that usually means that it's a respectable chain that's a decent place to stay overnight for business conferences. As we walked into the lobby with our bags in tow, the bright afternoon sun was high in the sky, but evening would be upon us soon. Chloe and I both got checked in without any trouble and were immediately given keys to our second-floor rooms, which were right next door to each other.

When I got to my room, I discovered that it was clean and organized, the best you can hope for in a hotel. After walking in, I put my suitcase next to the overpriced mini bar so that it would be out of the way. Then I took off my shoes, pulled off the bed's comforter, and flopped down on the mattress. That always feels amazing. I wasted no time in finding the remote and surfing my way through the channels. Since there was no on-screen TV guide, that meant I had to find something the old fashion way. About halfway through, I found some old episodes of *South Park* and kept it there for a few hours until it was time for dinner. Since I didn't feel like going anywhere, I ordered a pizza and had it delivered. To my pleasant surprise, it came right on time. As soon as I closed the door, I wasted no time in devouring it.

About an hour later, I was relaxing before bed when I remembered that Chloe was next door. I couldn't help but wonder what she was doing. Staying in a hotel must be nothing to her anymore. But to me, I felt like I was staying in a foreign place. I'd have to ask her if she had any tips for sleeping well in a hotel in the morning. Switching off the lights, I got into bed and eventually slipped into an uneasy sleep.

†

I kept it simple at breakfast; some eggs, hash browns, and coffee. The eggs were so rubbery they could be a dog's chew toy, but the tater tots were hot and crispy. Since the only thing I hate more than cold tater tots is cold pizza, it wasn't a bad deal. After jumping in the shower, I met Chloe out in the lobby and we headed out.

"Good night's sleep?" I asked as we walked out into the bright morning sunshine.

"Not bad, you?"

"Eh, it was ok," I answered as I unlocked my car. "You have directions to Mrs. Hanson's house?"

"Sure do."

†

After a short drive, I wound up parking beside a Chinese restaurant. The kind with Christmas lights in the front window and a generic sounding name that changes with every new owner. We made our way to a red ranch house with a bug zapper on the front porch. Its sickly blue glow flickered lazily as we rang the doorbell. Standing on the cluttered front porch, I could hear footsteps from inside before the door swung open.

"Chloe Vale, I've been expecting you." The woman I assumed was Mrs. Hanson swept her up in a hug. She was dressed in worn out blue jeans and an oversized red knit sweater.

"Hi Mrs. Hanson, good to see you."

"Oh sweetie, you know you can call me Barb."

"I know, but old habits die hard. You will always be Mrs. Hanson to me."

"I know that feeling," she affectionately agreed. Mrs. Hanson then took a step back from Chloe to get a closer look at me.

"Vince O'Malley, nice to meet you." I introduced myself while reaching out to shake her hand. When she reciprocated, I noticed that she had quite a firm grip.

Mrs. Hanson looked like the teacher who scolded you for sharpening your pencil during class. The same one who chain-smoked in the teachers' lounge during lunch. She was a shorter woman, about 5'5", but had what you would call presence. Her piercing grey eyes and slender nose were framed by black hair that I could tell had been recently colored and permed. But when she looked at me, I could see her eyes weren't harsh.

"Lovely to meet you. I've been expecting you both. Please come inside," she beckoned us as she headed back indoors. "Make yourselves comfortable, I just need to grab something from the kitchen," she added.

"Does it feel weird being inside your teacher's house?" I asked Chloe as Mrs. Hanson disappeared into the kitchen.

"It does feel odd," she admitted. "Half the time your teachers are like your parents when you are younger. You can't see them as anything else but a detached authority figure. It's why seeing a teacher out in public when you're a kid is so weird. It's like peering behind the curtain and seeing the real person."

"That is so true."

Mrs. Hanson's sitting room looked exactly how I'd imagined an old teacher's house would look; small and neat but filled with various trinkets and knickknacks. Souvenirs from a career filled with students sucking up for a good grade and genuinely grateful students and their parents. I counted several porcelain apples and pencil-shaped bookends on the mantelpiece alone. I could imagine her grading papers with a red sharpie while perched on one of the living room's comfortable couches, the TV blaring on in the background.

"Please have a seat, you two," Mrs. Hanson hustled back from the kitchen. "Welcome to my home. It's good to see you Chloe, been a long time hasn't it?"

"Yes, it sure has Mrs. Hanson," Chloe replied before making herself comfortable on the couch. "Good to see you too."

"And just who is this handsome young man?" she asked while looking at me. "Your boyfriend?"

"He used to date Allison," came Chloe's hasty answer. Mrs. Hanson immediately shook her head and sighed when Allison's name was mentioned. I couldn't help but notice how Chloe didn't answer the woman's question, but she didn't deny it either.

"Such a shame about her. But I wasn't surprised when I found out what happened. Her mother did the same thing once."

"Did what once?" I was puzzled, but I had a feeling that she had something big to tell us.

"Tried to kill herself. Although Mrs. Dunbar wasn't successful at it. But then again, she never really wanted to be either. You know the old saying about people who say they want to hurt themselves?" We both nodded that we did. "In her case, Claire Dunbar wanted attention from her husband. Had she truly wanted to end it all, she would've known how to do that as a doctor's daughter."

"That makes sense. Was that what made her husband want a divorce?" I asked the older woman.

"It was part of it no doubt. It was all kept very quiet around here. Frank Ballard, our principal back then, told me that the Dunbars were leaving town for a family emergency. That was in about 2004 and Allison was taken out of school for a little while. Months later, a nurse I knew at the local hospital confirmed it. Claire tried to swallow a bunch of pills."

Goose bumps began snaking their way up my arms. She must have known what her mother had done. Even if she didn't know at the time, Allison must have figured it out later as she got older. Chloe looked like she had just swallowed something incredibly unpleasant.

"Do you know what triggered it?" I continued.

"I do not. Many people out there are predisposed to hurting themselves, be it through booze, drugs, or any other risky behavior. Some people just need death to be closing in on them in order to feel alive. But I can tell you that in the months preceding the incident, Allison's work in class had suffered. She was actually a pretty good student when she set her mind to it." Mrs. Hanson's demeanor changed as she uttered the last thought. She now had the forlorn expression of someone wondering about how different things could have been.

"Chloe, did Allison ever mention her mother attempting something like that before?" I asked in a surprisingly calm voice. She steadied herself with a deep breath before answering.

"After I had known her a while, she mentioned in passing that her mother had a bad reaction to some medication and had to go to the hospital. That happened in a previous place they lived." Her voice was even, but her eyes told me that she felt the same as Mrs. Hanson.

I suddenly remembered those messages asking me if I missed Allison and whatever. Was her death in the hospital not her first attempt? I didn't know, but it seemed likely. At this point, it seems that Allison was far more dangerous to herself than she ever was to me. Mrs. Hanson suddenly sat upright in her chair. I could tell the old teacher was getting ready to deliver an important lesson.

"No matter how old a former student becomes, we can't help but always see them as the child in our class. For better or worse, we never forget our students as we knew them." She fiddled with the antique locket around her neck before continuing. "Allison," she spoke the name with a slow deliberateness, "was a very interesting girl. I will never forget the day she stepped foot into my classroom. She was one of those girls who just got your attention. She also had her own unique way of interacting with others."

"What do you mean by that?"

"You ever see documentaries of tribes living out in the jungle?"

"Of course," I said, momentarily surprised by the question.

"You don't understand what exactly they're saying, but if you pay close enough attention you can figure out the pecking order. Who sits where and with who. They have their own rituals. That's what teaching can be like." Now I knew exactly what she meant. Like in real estate, one rule of power is that location is everything.

"So, what did you observe?" I asked.

"Times may change, but human nature doesn't. Allison grew up watching her mother being put on a pedestal and doing whatever she pleased. I believe deference is the best word that describes it. Allison's family was used to a certain level of deference from their peers. Or at least it started out as deference."

"What did it turn into?" While Chloe continued to sit silently on the couch, she was by no means disengaged from our conversation. I knew she was taking in her old teacher's every word.

"Jealousy. Something else I've learned from teaching is that power is like mountain climbing; the higher you go, the more perilous the ascent becomes. In an animal kingdom, there is always another rival waiting for their chance to become top dog."

"Who wanted to take Mrs. Dunbar's place?" Mrs. Hanson responded with an amused chuckle.

"More like who didn't want to take her place. The worst offenders were her 'friends' who smiled the widest and praised her the loudest. But she managed to stay on her golden perch for long enough. Too long in most people's opinion."

"How did she hold power over people?"

"People try to get power in any form they can. Kids will pick on each other for a pathetic reason. But it's just a means of putting someone down for your own gain. That's it. Kids are vicious that way and adults can be uncannily similar. Claire could be a pain in the ass perfectionist about the annual gala, or a thousand other trivial matters. Know why?"

"To remind people that they had flaws and she saw all of them." The phrase made me think of all the times Allison could be a real bitch at the drop of a hat. It wasn't a pleasant feeling.

"Good man," she said before turning to Chloe. "Your decision to talk to him was an excellent one," she added, seeming rather pleased with herself. She leaned back in her chair before addressing us both again.

"She would let people know in her passive aggressive way that she knew their baggage as well. That she felt so bad that your husband was fucking the waitress at the café on Elm and what a scumbag he was and that your secret was safe with her."

"But she never kept it quiet, did she?"

"Funny enough, most times she actually did. Unless she wanted to let it slip for a reason, Claire knew how to make good use of people's private humiliations. If you spill someone's secret, that means you don't have that power over them anymore. But eventually she had her own situation to deal with. Her brother."

"What happened to him?"

"No one around here really knows for certain. People whispered rumors all over town and they ran the gauntlet from amusing to downright outrageous."

"I didn't know Allison had an uncle," Chloe replied.

"That's no surprise. He was the kind of uncle you don't talk about in polite company. No, not that kind." Mrs. Hanson added when she saw our reaction. "It's sad to say, but had he been a friendly uncle, Allison's mother probably wouldn't have cared so long as he didn't risk the family status." I felt a sick lurch in my chest as she said this.

"What did he do?" I asked.

"He got mixed up in some nasty business. My late husband was a cop and he knew from some contacts that Allison's uncle had a history of ties with unsavory people. There was some shady business deal and it ended with the wrong people not getting their money. As often happens in these matters, someone ended up dead and Claire's brother needed a lawyer. A damn good one. The kind with a Mercedes and a bad spray tan."

"That's crazy," Chloe mumbled quietly.

"Oh wait, there's more. From what I know, he could have been Jack the Ripper and Claire wouldn't have cared so long as he didn't get caught. But now he had broken the longstanding rule about not endangering the family image."

"Nice priorities." Chloe was so disgusted she practically spat the last word out.

"Many people pretend to be something they're not. Hell, a lot of times people openly encourage it for the sake of status. The problems come when a façade crumbles, which it always does in the end."

"And when you can't pretend anymore, people turn on you." I knew exactly what she was talking about.

"That's right. So, what do you do when that illusion is at risk of falling apart?"

"Depends on what exactly is being threatened I guess." I shrugged my arms. "What exactly was at stake?"

"Not just the family image, which was paramount, but it's financial standing as well. In a place like Maple Bluffs, you can have status without money and keep your influence. Or you can have money without prestige and be respected, but losing both money and respectability is fatal. It's why so many 'old money types' are really broke, but no one cares."

"Their name is their asset. You need at least the appearance of wealth," Chloe finished.

"Bingo," Mrs. Hanson said while wagging her finger in a gesture of approval.

"But Mrs. Dunbar wasn't wrong, was she, Mrs. Hanson?" I added.

"Nope. Even a broken clock is right twice a day. Claire knew better than anyone that people willingly tolerate almost anything except failure. It comes in many forms, but if you look at history, your own relationships, and general human behavior, people are merciless towards what they perceive as failure."

That was one of the most intelligent things anyone has ever said to me. Napoleon was one of the most brilliant military leaders in European history and his battlefield victories changed warfare as we know it. But his notorious defeat at Waterloo overshadowed all that.

"So, when the old image fails, you either create a new façade or move somewhere people will buy the old one," I concluded.

"Well done, my boy. In a city with a million people, no one would have cared about Claire's brother. But here, gossip is its own little black market. It fuels everything. It lurks behind every corner like some boogieman, waiting to devour the next victim. Anyways, her brother was found dead in a trailer a while later. The thing caught fire when he was taking a nap inside it. That was about the same time Allison's father was last heard from."

My hands tightened on the arm of the sofa when I heard that he died in a fire, just like one unfortunate paramedic.

"Mrs. Arlington says that not only did he want custody of Allison specifically, he disappeared after saying he would check back in with her after Mrs. Dunbar's trip to see her mother."

"Who's Mrs. Arlington?" Mrs. Hanson asked.

"My neighbor. Turns out she knew Allison's father. Did you know a legal secretary named Sharon who used to work for a lawyer in town?"

"Vaguely. She was a nice lady. Why do you ask?"

"According to her, Allison's father was worried about his wife and he disappeared after Mrs. Dunbar went to visit her mother. She said that Mrs. Dunbar absolutely hated her."

"Oh yeah, no love ever contaminated the relationship between Claire Dunbar and Silvia,"

"I can't remember Allison ever talking about her grandmother," Chloe agreed. "Every time it came up, Allison would change the subject. That was the same grandmother that Mrs. Dunbar took out a big life insurance policy for right before her husband disappeared."

"Oh shit," was all Mrs. Hanson could say. "That's not good."

"Do you know anything about her grandmother?" I asked while shifting my weight on the seat.

"Just that she and her daughter didn't get along," Mrs. Hanson replied. "Wish I knew more."

"From what I know, the two were a lot alike," Chloe said.

"That wouldn't surprise me. People who are a lot alike are either mortal enemies or the best of friends."

"Allison did once mention to me that her grandma's bridge club knew more about what was going on in their old town than the police did," I remembered suddenly.

"Allison's grandfather was a doctor, right?" Mrs. Hanson asked Chloe.

"Yes," she confirmed.

"That explains it. Back in the day, doctors knew everything that went down in small towns."

"Speaking of knowing everything, what do you know about Allison's father?"

"You actually remind me a bit of him, Vince. He was a straight shooter and I always liked him, unlike his wife. But he was in over his head, as any of us would be in his situation."

"How?"

"For starters, he was the kind of guy who always tried to see the best in others. Which made him a sitting duck for someone like his wife."

"So, what changed his attitude?"

"I don't know if anything truly changed. I think Mr. Dunbar just realized that something had been amiss for a while. It just became obvious."

"I know that feeling," I muttered quietly. Mrs. Hanson smiled sympathetically at me before continuing.

"From what my husband told me and what I can piece together, Claire's brother disappeared about the same time Mr. Dunbar was getting suspicious, so it's fair to say that's what probably broke the camel's back. I remember seeing him around town and his entire demeanor had changed. It was like he was looking at everything differently."

There was another feeling I knew all too well. Mrs. Hanson briefly tugged on one of her gold clip-on earrings before resuming her story.

"I sure would've been worried if I was him. While I can't say why he seemed to disappear, I can tell you what I heard. Everyone had a theory they were happy to share, especially after the Dunbars left town. The favorite was that he left town for another woman and Claire moved to escape the shame. A close second was that he did business with the wrong people and he disappeared in order to pay the piper."

"What do you think?" I asked, taking care to emphasize the 'you'. She took a deep breath before answering.

"I believe someone did business with the wrong people all right, but it wasn't him. I think it was something ugly and big enough to rattle him. I also think Claire knew about what was on his mind and perhaps did something about it."

"That makes sense, since someone knew he and Mrs. Arlington were going through her stuff when she was out of the house." I felt my throat tighten up as I recalled this.

"Whether she did it herself or not, Claire is responsible for her husband's disappearance. You see, she never wanted to actually die from taking too many pills. That was all a bid for power in the form of attention and leverage. It happens all the time, especially when someone is desperate to keep a significant other from leaving. Just like in that movie with Glenn Close and Michael Douglas."

I knew exactly what movie she meant. It was *Fatal Attraction*, a movie I could probably do without seeing again for a long time. As I remembered it, a cold chill shot up my back. Was that why Allison took all those pills in the hospital? Was it angst over Millstone, a man who didn't want her anymore?

"It's like when a kid runs away to make their parents all worried about them," Chloe added as I was wrestling with my thoughts.

"That's exactly right. Now if you two will excuse me, I have to use the bathroom. It's these new damn pills they have me on."

She left us in what seemed like deafening silence. I looked at Chloe, but she looked just as stunned as I was. Since I had no idea what to say to her, I stared intently at the lush red carpeting on the floor. Before we knew it, Mrs. Hanson was walking back towards us.

"So, where was I?" she asked rhetorically as she resumed her seat. "Long after the fact, my husband did some research on Allison's grandfather. It turns out that he got into a bit of trouble himself. Seemed he was a bit, oh what's the word, generous with prescriptions. Morphine in particular."

"Oh shit." I practically shuddered at this latest bit of information.

"Oh shit is right. Fortunately for him, things were a lot different back then. It was kept quiet and he got off with a slap on the wrist. I don't know if he stopped or just didn't get caught again."

"I bet he just didn't get caught again," Chloe muttered absentmindedly.

"I would suspect the same," Mrs. Hanson agreed.

"Let me get this straight," I began. "Allison's father disappeared about the same time her uncle, who was risking the family's false reputation and status, suddenly died."

"Correct. I believe Chloe has told you a bit about their wealth?"

"Yes."

"They lived in one of the nicest houses in town. Over on Belmont Avenue. It's still there in fact. Hasn't been occupied in years, and I suspect people may be too afraid to demolish it."

"Speaking of their house, Mrs. Arlington says that she got some phone calls after Allison's father disappeared. It was mostly heavy breathing, but she was told in no uncertain terms to leave the Dunbar matter alone. They even knew she had been at their house."

"Then it's true," Mrs. Hanson concluded with a touch of sadness. "They really did have connections to some unsavory people. I don't know if you know this, but for years Missouri was the meth capital of the Country."

"No, I didn›t.»

"Well, Allison's uncle didn't just die in a fire; he died in a fire caused by an explosion. It seemed that he and another guy were trying to either make or consume meth. None of this got out, but my husband managed to get ahold of it."

"Why didn't it get out?"

"Another meth explosion in a trailer with a few dead users is not exactly breaking news. The fact that he didn't have the Dunbar name also helped a lot."

"That makes sense."

"You asked how Claire confronted the issue of her brother. Well, the truth of the matter is that she just didn't react. Publicly at least. Although if people did find out, Claire would have made them feel sorry for her. That's how clever she was. I do have to give her that; she was a clever one. Way smarter than most people around here. Her husband was no fool, but she was miles ahead of him."

"On that note, I met Allison when she was the manager of a bar. After she died, they started looking into the place and according to the official paperwork, the registered owner is her mother."

"Interesting, but that doesn't surprise me at all. I could easily see her putting her daughter up as the pretty girl drawing people in while she was the one running the show from behind the scenes. That's pretty much how she was around here."

"Fair enough. She sort of fell apart after we broke up."

"I see. Why did you guys break up?"

"She cheated on me and had developed a drug problem."

"I'm so sorry," she responded immediately, emphasizing the *so* as she spoke.

"Thank you."

"As you can tell, drug problems aren't exactly uncommon in her family and where there's substance abuse, infidelity usually isn't far behind. On that note, I think Claire Dunbar didn't have the slightest concern about her husband, but she also couldn't abide someone leaving her or the implications that might have." I knew what Mrs. Hanson meant all too well. Allison didn't give two shits about me until I was the one who ended things.

"Even rotten apples don't fall far from the tree," I felt myself blurt out. Mrs. Hanson smiled as if I had just given her some treat.

"I like you, Vince," she added with a brief smile. "I want you to know that, as well as the fact that I genuinely want you to do well and be safe. Chloe wanted my opinion, so here it is. While the stuff about Allison's father or uncle is troubling, that's not what scares me." Mrs. Hanson wearily removed her eye glasses and looked genuinely worried for the first time since we arrived. "What scares me is all the stuff we don't know. Because I won't lie to you, I think there's more where that came from. A lot more."

"Thanks, Mrs. Hanson," I managed to respond. "If Chloe has nothing else left to ask, I think it's time we headed out."

Chloe nodded in agreement before we both gave her a goodbye hug. When it was my turn, she whispered "Take good care of her and be careful, especially in this town," into my ear.

"I will."

"Good."

By now the humid morning had given way to what seemed like a balmy afternoon. But as Chloe and I walked silently to the car, there was definitely a chill in the air.

18

We drove back to the hotel in silence. I mean really, after revelations like that, what is there to say? Glancing at myself in the rearview mirror, I looked ok; a bit tired perhaps, but ok nonetheless. Chloe on the other hand, was slumped down low in her chair, nervously twirling a strand of hair around her finger over and over again. After about five minutes of silence, Chloe suddenly came to life.

"Keep going straight down this road until you reach the Goodwill."

I did as Chloe asked and when I reached the Goodwill, she told me to take a right, which led down a backroad patterned with potholes. The road snaked around an overgrown cluster of spruce trees before it straightened out and delivered us in front of a neat row of houses. Looking around, I had an idea about why we were here. This wasn't some cookie-cutter development of McMansions freshly built for the newly rich. No, these were old, fairly well preserved houses for the crème de la crème of Maple Bluffs. Driving slowly down the street, I noticed that virtually every house had blinds closed or curtains drawn, which meant that I wasn't sure which houses were occupied and which ones were empty. Or perhaps they were all empty. Either way, I felt like an unwanted intruder. As my gaze lingered over each house, I was waiting for the blinds to snap open and reveal someone leering at us with an unblinking stare and lecherous smile. But that never happened. We were about halfway down the street when Chloe spoke up.

"That used to be her house." She pointed out a neat grey colonial with Greek style columns on either side of the front door. "We used to live right there," she added while indicating the house to the right. It was a neat red Victorian with ivy steadily winding its way up the front porch. I lingered in front of the two houses for about two minutes before putting the car in park.

"Do you want to go inside?" I asked.

"No, believe me, I've spent quite enough time in both houses as it is. I thought seeing this again would make me think, you know? Recall something I'd forgotten."

"Did it work?"

"Sort of. I remembered how many antiques they used to have. But what really came flooding back to me is the smell. Their house always smelled amazing because of all the flowers Mrs. Dunbar kept around. She loved gardening and used to keep a little greenhouse in the back for all her best flowers. I remember Allison's favorite flower was some red one that I never knew the name of. But if I saw it today, I would probably recognize it."

"Interesting. Mrs. Arlington loves to garden too, every summer she grows vegetables in a little garden she keeps by her back porch. Was Mrs. Dunbar any good at it?"

"Very. She won a bunch of awards and even scored second place one year at the state fair."

"Second place huh? Bet she hated that."

"You bet she did. She always maintained that the reason she came in second was because the woman who won first slept with all the judges."

"Charming."

"I know. We can leave now if you like."

"Cool."

†

We ended up stopping at the nearest Pizza Hut for lunch. Over the pepperoni and green pepper pizza we split, Chloe was very subdued and didn't say much. I could tell she was still stuck on what Mrs. Hanson had told us. I couldn't blame her, because finding out that events from the past were a series of lies agreed upon by those around you is a dreadful thing to swallow. It reduces you to micro analyzing every little detail you can remember, slowly driving you crazy in the process. Finding out what happened to Allison in no way affected my childhood memories. But for Chloe, those were things that quite literally happened in her own backyard. A revelation like that makes you question what you think is reality. What happened to Allison was in no way her fault, but guilt can be a curious thing. Compounding things is the fact that those who blame themselves usually don't deserve it and those who should blame themselves absolutely refuse to.

"It's not your fault, you know," I offered after finishing my second slice of pizza

"What's not my fault?" she asked while taking a sip of her drink.

"Allison. Whatever happened to her here is in no way your fault and there is nothing you could have done to change it."

"Thanks. Was it that obvious?"

"To someone else, probably not. But to me, yes. I've been there before, however briefly."

"You have indeed."

"I also feel compelled to point out how significant historical events are often the result of accidents. Or a series of accidents."

"Oh yeah, like how? Give me an example, professor."

"JFK had a history of back problems. He would sometimes wear a back brace for certain events like campaigning. On November 22, 1963 he was wearing one while riding through a motorcade in Dallas. He was shot twice; once in the lower neck and once in the head. Since he was wearing the back brace, he didn't automatically go down after being hit in the neck and was kept upright for the headshot. Since it was ruled that the neck wound wasn't fatal, his back brace arguably killed him."

"Wow, that is crazy to think," she agreed after taking another bite of pizza.

"But my personal favorite is this one. While in Florida right before taking office, some crazy tried to kill Franklin Roosevelt while he was shaking hands with the Mayor of Chicago. Some woman there saw what was going down and whacked the gunman's arm with her purse. The dude's aim got all fucked up and he hit the Mayor instead. If he had hit FDR, the entire 20th Century would have been different. Just ask Phillip K. Dick."

"Who?"

"An author who wrote an entire book based on the premise. FDR dying early is the one historical event he altered that set off a chain of events which lead to a Nazi victory during World War II. They recently made it into an Amazon series."

"Was it any good?"

"Yeah, it was."

"Good. That's a fascinating idea, but it doesn't surprise me. People love to endlessly recreate the past and wonder 'what if?' regarding their own history, so it's not surprising they would do the exact same thing to human history."

"Exactly."

"Thanks, Vince, I feel better now," she said. I could tell she was sincere; her entire demeanor now seemed lighter. Years of teaching in a classroom helps you get a feel for someone's mood even when they're just sitting there.

"You're welcome."

We finished most of the pizza and went back to the hotel after that. When I walked in my room, I promptly turned on the TV and crashed on the bed, where I slept fitfully for a few hours. Waking up, I slowly became reacquainted with my surroundings and realized how thirsty I was. But that wasn't a surprise. Takeout pizza usually makes you thirsty, especially if you get something like pepperoni on it, which contains a lot of salt.

Grabbing a glass from the room's wooden table, I walked into the bathroom and flipped on the lights. Quickly filling the glass under the tap, I downed it in a series of gulps. It may have been lukewarm, but it tasted amazing to me. After I filled it a second time, I drank most of it and felt satisfied. My thirst having been quenched, I watched some more TV before deciding to treat myself. Since this was technically a vacation, I decided to get room service and a pay per view movie. I checked my appearance in the mirror before I left the room and walked next door, where I announced my presence by knocking on Chloe's door.

I didn't get an answer, but the door swung open to reveal a haze of shower humidity. Like most hotels, the rooms here all seemed to have the bathroom right next to the front door. On the other side of the doorway, Chloe greeted me in a white terrycloth bathrobe while drying her hair with a matching towel.

"Hey, I'm gonna get some room service and order a movie. Want to join me?"

"I'd like that, just give me one sec and I'll figure out what I want to eat, ok?"

"Sure."

Walking back to my room, I faintly realized that apart from the bathrobe, Chloe was probably completely naked. Shoving that thought aside, I left the door slightly ajar before flipping through the pay per view selections to see what to watch. I decided on *No Country for Old Men*, which was based on a book I really loved. It didn't hurt that I also happen to enjoy most movies made by the Coen Brothers. Chloe came by soon after that, dressed comfortably in a white tank top and jean shorts.

"Can I see the menu?" she asked before kicking off her flip flops and jumping on the bed, settling right next to me. As she did, I caught a whiff of her perfume; the kind that is guaranteed to come in a neon pink bottle with bright gold lettering. I could also feel that she was still warm from the shower, the humidity faintly radiating off her skin.

"Of course." I offered her the room's black binder. "You mind if we watch this movie?"

"No, it's fine." She briefly looked up from browsing the menu to glance at the TV. "What are you getting?"

"The crispy chicken sandwich and fries."

"Cool, I'll take the house salad."

After ordering the food and starting the movie, I leaned back against the headboard and put my feet up on the bed. Next to me, Chloe crossed her legs yoga style and put a pillow on her lap, resting her arms on top of it. Our food arrived right on time 30 minutes later. I always appreciate it when my order is prepared on time, so I made sure to give the hotel guy a decent tip. I rarely ever eat food in bed, so this was unusual for me. Like most room service, the food was decent, but considerably overpriced. But that's the price of convenience.

"So, what's it like being back?" I asked Chloe after we had eaten and were back to relaxing on the bed. She paused, resting her hand underneath her chin.

"I wouldn't say it's good. Even if this place was filled with good memories, your home is never just good."

"Right."

"But we have learned a lot being here."

"Can't argue with that."

"And I have good company, so that's definitely a plus," she added before giving me a kiss on the cheek.

We didn't say anything else for the rest of the movie. Towards the end, I noticed her getting a bit sleepy. Before long, she quietly laid down next to me and went to sleep. It was rather endearing. I channel surfed through some bad television before I switched it off and quietly crept off the bed and went to the bathroom, where I brushed my teeth and got changed for bed. When I opened the bathroom door as quietly as possible, I saw I hadn't disturbed her. Good. With a flick of the light switch, the room went completely dark. I let my eyes adjust to it before I crawled back into bed next to Chloe.

Because of my long nap earlier, I figured it would take a while to get to sleep. While I stared up at the ceiling, the air conditioner under the window churned away, making the heavy window drapes shimmer faintly back and forth. Like most people, I never open the curtains while staying in a hotel room. Unless you have a fantastic view or something, it just feels weird, you know? Turning over on my side, I made sure to adjust the sheets a bit so Chloe would be comfortable. Not gonna lie, I felt much better having her here. I hated feeling like I was alone in some bland hotel room in a city I didn't know and certainly didn't like much.

Eventually, I felt myself begin to drift back and forth into sleep. The next thing I knew, I was awake in a room that was slightly less dark than it had been earlier. Rolling over to look at the alarm clock on the bedside table, I saw 8:42 in large red numbers. On the other side of the bed where

Chloe had been, a note written on a piece of paper containing the hotel logo was in her place.

"Hey sleepy, I went next door to shower and get dressed. I'll meet you back here and we can go down to breakfast together before we check out."

I hopped in the bathroom for a quick shower and got dressed in grey jeans and a red button up. Unless I am really tired or sore, I generally don't like to linger in the shower forever like some people do. I was just grabbing my wallet when there was a gentle knock at the door.

"Hey, if you're the hot chick I hooked up with last night, I told you already, I won't be your sugar daddy."

"Very funny," I could practically hear Chloe rolling her eyes from the other side of the door.

"I thought it was," I replied as I stepped into the hotel hallway. While Chloe always looked great, she looked especially good this morning; her aquamarine t-shirt and tight black yoga pants vividly contrasted with the hotel's blandly patterned carpet and faded off-white walls.

"Ready to head downstairs?"

"You got it." I made sure I had my room key before shutting the door behind me. As we walked together to the elevator, Chloe's flip flops announced her every step.

"Did you sleep well?" I asked after stepping inside the small carpeted elevator.

"I did, actually. You?"

"Not bad. Better than the first night."

"Me too. Wonder why that was." She winked at me cheekily.

"Yeah, that is a mystery. You hogged all the blankets, so that made it way harder to sleep."

"Lies, and I'm amazed I could sleep with you snoring like a hibernating bear with sleep apnea."

"Now who's lying?"

By now the elevator had dropped us off on the first floor. The hotel's sitting room where the continental breakfast was being held was pleasantly quiet with few people there. I grabbed some scrambled eggs and french toast, while Chloe helped herself to pancakes and hash browns. I was surprisingly hungry, and in what seemed like no time at all, we were finished and heading back upstairs in the elevator.

"Checkout time is at noon, so we have about two hours to kill. Anything you want to do," was all I could get out before Chloe's lips were on mine.

I stumbled back slightly in surprise, bumping into the rear of the elevator as I did. But Chloe didn't miss a beat. She just wrapped her arms around my neck in response and nibbled my lower lip. It felt amazing. Last time she kissed me it had been great too, but this was different. I instinctively wrapped my arms around her waist and we held that pose for what seemed like a few moments. Before I knew it, she had grabbed my hand and we were heading back to my room. As I fumbled clumsily for the room key in my pocket, she laughed.

"Having a little trouble with the key there, bud?"

"Nope, got it." I dragged the key out and opened the door triumphantly. As I shoved it open, I grabbed Chloe's hand and led her inside.

"I was wondering if you'd be into this. Been wondering since we checked in. I didn't want to even consider it unless I was sure you wanted to and were ready for it."

Her sincerity and concern for my welfare was quite touching. I didn't say anything, but I smiled at her and grabbed the Do Not Disturb sign from the back of the door and hung it on the front end of the doorknob, the door clicking shut as I was turning back to face her.

19

"Why?" was the first thing I said while we were lazily sprawled across the bed. I hadn't felt this good in a long time and I didn't hear any complaints from Chloe either. Quite the opposite, in fact.

"Why?" she repeated slowly as she looked sideways at me while nestled against my left side. "That was the first thing I kept asking myself about you when we met. Why in the hell would Allison toss a guy like you out like last week's leftovers? It drove me insane. As I got to know you better, it only got worse. But when I started to remember everything I knew about her, I wasn't surprised. Allison could never make anything last, especially if it was something worthwhile. She just didn't have the determination. But the simple answer to your question is because I really like you a lot and have thought about this for a long time."

"Awww, that's so sweet." I tilted my head down and kissed her forehead.

"It also doesn't hurt that you're in good shape," she muttered after laying her head under my neck.

"Yeah, well you aren't exactly lacking in that department either." We laid there a while before she said the phrase I was expecting, but still didn't want to hear.

"Come on, we need to head out."

While we were both in our respective rooms packing up and making sure we had everything, I noticed that I had a missed call from Ramsay. His voicemail politely requested I call him back as soon as I could.

"Hey Detective, it's me," I began when he picked up on the second ring.

"Vince, thanks for calling. Got some news for you. I heard back from an old contact of mine and you will love this. The bar Allison ran for her mother is being investigated for money laundering. It seems like the place is a front."

"For what, drugs?"

"Yup. Apparently the state and the feds have been keeping their eye on the place for a long time."

"What do we do now?"

"Sit tight and see if there is anything else you can think of. You guys have been doing fantastically well."

"I appreciate that. I just wish I could figure out why the hell that guy looks familiar."

"You will. You're a smart guy Vince, I have no doubt you will figure it out."

"That means a lot to me. We're on our way back today."

"Good I'm glad. Did you guys manage ok out there?"

"Yeah, we did fine," I felt my face grow hot. "We found out that the Dunbar family has a long history of unsavory behavior."

"No surprise there. We'll talk more when you get back. Drive safe and see you soon."

I couldn't help but suspect that although he didn't say a word or even hint at it, Ramsay knew why I had missed his call. If that was true, I was infinitely grateful he didn't say a word about it. A few moments later, Chloe came into my room to see if I was ready to check out. I told her I was and repeated what Ramsay told me.

"We're getting somewhere," was all she had to say before we rolled our suitcases out of the rooms, down the hallway, and into the elevator. On the way down to the lobby, I couldn't help but smile as I thought about our previous ride in it.

The middle-aged woman at the front desk helped us check out quickly. Before I knew it, she was saying "Thank you for staying with us and have a safe trip." After tossing our bags into the trunk of my car, we hopped in the front seat and I maneuvered out of the parking lot and back onto the highway. When we passed the sign welcoming us to Maple Bluffs, I felt lighter. As I watched it fade away into the distance, I felt a sense of fun come over me. Since it was a beautiful day out and I was in a great mood, I rolled down the windows and turned the radio up. Somehow even the trees and grass bordering the highway seemed greener than before.

"Someone's in a good mood," Chloe observed amusedly from the passenger seat after we had been driving for about an hour.

"Hey, why shouldn't I be?" I turned down the radio as a Springsteen song finished.

"This is true." We were well back into Illinois by now. That's the one great thing about trips; the journey home always seems to take much less time.

"Any preferences for lunch?" I asked while the car radio clock steadily inched towards 2 pm.

"No, I'll let you pick."

"Good deal. Anything you're allergic to or just won't eat?"

"I don't do shellfish. Something about the way they look just bothers me."

"I feel you. Live lobsters look downright creepy. Like spiders."

"That's part of it. But I do eat fish and stuff."

"Mrs. Arlington will like that. She's a huge fan of Red Lobster. It's her favorite place to go."

"She's such a sweetheart. Does she have any family around here?"

"Unfortunately, no she doesn't. Her husband passed a while ago and her stepson from him is a real piece of shit."

"That's a shame,"

"It really is. Dude is a lowlife."

"You know him?"

"I never met him, but I've heard all about him. This will help you picture him; he was the relative that always looked awkward as hell in family photos. In one Christmas photo, it looked like he was being held for ransom. The only thing missing was the newspaper with the current date on it."

"That's hilarious."

"It was good. In fact, I think I still have it somewhere. Mrs. Arlington emailed me a bunch of pictures a year ago, wanting to know which ones looked good enough to keep in a scrapbook or something. I'll see if I can find it when we get something to eat."

We ended up stopping at a Five Guys for lunch. Since I was in a good mood, I decided to indulge in a chocolate milkshake. I even shared the silver mixing container with the leftover ice cream with Chloe. While we were waiting for the bill, I went through my email to see if I could find the picture I mentioned to her. I was about four pictures through the slide show when it felt like the milkshake had just turned to ice in my chest. I finally realized why that one guy Ramsay showed me looked so familiar. He may have been several years younger and had a full head of hair this time, but there he was, sitting right next to Mrs. Arlington and her husband in their old house.

†

Ramsay was absolutely floored when I gave him the news. He told me in no uncertain terms that he would take it from here and would contact Mrs. Arlington himself. I was grateful for that; because while I should have been thrilled that I figured out who that guy was, all I felt was an unpleasant emptiness. It seemed like an eternity had passed since this morning.

The rest of the drive home passed in a rush. I was dashing past exits as quickly as I could. Finally, the exit to get off by my duplex came up and I was roaring down the street. Squealing to a halt in front of my house, I flung open the driver's side door and rushed to Mrs. Arlington's front porch. But before I could even start knocking, the front door opened. Sharon Arlington had always looked and acted younger than she was, but this was the first time ever that she truly looked older to me. While I had always felt bad on her behalf about the Morgan situation, that sympathy had just reached a new level.

"I'm sorry just doesn't seem to cut it about Morgan anymore." I murmured as I gave her a hug.

"Oh honey, it's not your fault." She sounded so exhausted as she spoke. "If anything, I should say that to you. There is no telling what Morgan had to do with Allison."

"We'll find out soon enough,"

"Sad thing is, I knew something like this would happen. I KNEW that one day, I would get the call."

Chloe walked up to Mrs. Arlington and gave her a hug as well. Once we were inside her kitchen, she offered us coffee and said she had given Ramsay all of Morgan's personally identifiable info and he was putting out a search for him.

"They'll find him. I just know it." I had the feeling she was saying that more for her own sake than for Chloe's or mine. As we left Mrs. Arlington's, I stopped Chloe.

"You don't really want to go back to a hotel having already left one today, do you?"

"Eh, I don't mind, I'm used to it."

"Well I do and I feel like I've aged a year in three hours. You said it yourself that you slept better in my room. How about you stay here for a while?"

"You really mean that?" she asked hopefully.

"Absolutely. I'd like that a lot. I have plenty of room and could use the company."

"I would like that a lot too." She made herself right at home and in no time at all, it felt like Chloe had always been there.

As it happened, Mrs. Arlington was right. They found Morgan a few days later when he was driving erratically through southern Wisconsin; 79 in a 55 zone. I couldn't help but laugh at that. After all this time, it all came down to a speeding ticket. Typical. At 9:15 am on a warm Sunday morning, I received word from Ramsay that Morgan was being read his Miranda rights and was cooperating with the cops. But there was no word about what he was giving them or what he knew.

In the meantime, Chloe and I went out and did normal things to help distract us from the Morgan situation. I found out that she loved to people watch at the mall, browse through bookstores, and had been think-ing about getting a tattoo. A smaller one, perhaps between her shoulder blades or on her foot. I was beginning to get my mind off Morgan when I got a text from Ramsay a week later.

"Turn on the news. You'll know it when you find it."

That was all he said. Switching the TV on, it didn't take me long before I knew what he meant. Somewhere way west of here in Missouri, the DEA and other agencies had staged a major raid on some compound. In the corner of the screen, the news anchor was showing a picture of the woman who owned the property. Even if they hadn't said her name, I would have known exactly who it was. Mrs. Claire Dunbar. She looked eerily like her daughter, except for the eyes. She had intense eyes that looked like they could consume you at any moment.

"Come check this out," I called to Chloe. She walked in and immediately froze when she saw the TV screen, her jaw suspended in disbelief as she watched helicopters and news vans swarming the property. According to the news, it was on 15 acres and contained four trailers and two barns, with drug paraphernalia found in every single one. A fleet of black SUV's were also parked inside one of the barns. The main house itself was quite nice looking; a large red brick house with a double door entryway.

Three days later, Ramsay came by to talk to all three of us at the same time. I could tell by his tone of voice that he had something big. Over the phone, he said that Morgan had spilled a lot of dirt and was giving names of all the people he knew that got wrapped up in Allison's situation. In turn, they were all chomping at the bit to turn on each other. No honor amongst thieves indeed.

"Alright guys, here it is. I will tell you everything I can remember and if you have any questions, ask me when I'm done, ok?" Sitting in my living room, we agreed and Ramsay started talking.

Mrs. Dunbar was a heroin trafficker. One of the bigger ones in the Midwest. Morgan had stumbled into her operation by chance, doing a favor for a local guy he owed one to. The bar Allison worked at was just one of the fronts her mother had operated over the years. The newspaper and meatpacking plant Chloe had mentioned were also part of it. The newspaper was especially handy because it gave her an eye and ear on all local news and sources. The meat plant was used to harvest and ship the product. But it also came in handy for squaring loose ends, because people expect to find blood in a meatpacking plant, don't they?

Speaking of loose ends, one of the people Morgan gave up dirt on knew what happened to Jerry Dunbar. When he went out of town like Mrs. Arlington mentioned, he was following his wife when he was driving past a gorge. Well, a deer happened to leap into the road at the worst moment and Jerry hit it and went off the road and down the embankment. He died instantly and since his body was never recovered, it was never reported either. I felt bad for the guy across the board, but part of me felt that he deserved a more heroic end. Like he died in the middle of defending himself in a gunfight or something.

But Allison's fate was by far the worst of all. Morgan and the others from his crew had been bringing her stuffed toys to and from the hospital as a cover for moving drugs. They were brought to the hospital empty, left for a little while, and then taken back out by various clients or associates of Mrs. Dunbar under the pretense of visiting her daughter. What better place to get access to top notch painkillers and opiates than a hospital? In the meantime, Ramsay and his colleagues had the one stuffed toy left in Allison's apartment checked and it tested positive for drug residue.

Allison was a perfect front because if she acted odd or paranoid, that was just a side effect of her condition. Which was where Daniel Millstone came in. All he had to do was stash the goods into Allison's stuffed toys and leave it. Mrs. Dunbar gave the people Millstone worked for a cut of the action and presto, instant access to top shelf painkillers.

But Millstone began to feel guilty and took up drinking to suffocate his conscience. One night, he got really drunk and wound up dead. They were furious when he died, just like they were furious when Allison did herself in too. There was no foul play in either death because why kill off your prized asset? But hey, they call them painkillers for a reason. Ramsay added that Mrs. Dunbar was beside herself over Allison's death, but I tend to think that she was more upset over the lost arrangement. Her daughter really did lose her mind, but like many people in this day and age, she lost her sanity with help. Then people around her promptly wasted no time whatsoever in using her mental state to their advantage.

However, even a broken clock is right twice a day. Since paranoia is quite common in someone with either mental or substance abuse issues, she had been getting extremely paranoid. So, unbeknownst to anyone, she set up a camera in her apartment and when that guy got rough with her, she lost it. But before she officially checked out and went off the deep end, she gathered up the video footage of what happened and stashed it in the last place anyone would ever look; my house. Ramsay also says that because no one has said a word about threatening me, the note with the hangman and the name Daniel may have been a reference to someone else, as another Daniel was amongst the guys trying to cut a deal to testify against Mrs. Dunbar. Later, we found out that Allison herself had sent it, but it had gotten lost in the mail and was delayed in sending because of the horrible handwriting.

It's ironic really. It took Allison dying in a horrible manner, plus her mother getting busted to finally give her what she always wanted; massive sympathy and attention. The headlines started flying almost immediately.

"Heroin heiress used beautiful daughter as a drug mule!" screamed one.

"Mother from hell stashed drugs in daughter's hospital room," another one righteously condemned. Mrs. Dunbar's house was already known as the Painkiller Plantation.

But had Allison been alive for all this, people would have turned on her with just as much fury. I can practically see it now; they would call her the Heroin Heiress or some other catchy label ready made for TV. The pundits would have a field day pouring over every detail of her life or how she looked when being arraigned. Her mugshot would go viral like one of those so-called hot felons and at every arraignment, there would be an ever-present army of thirsty men with misspelled signs proclaiming their love for her. In terms of criminals who get marriage proposals, Allison would put Casey Anthony, Manson, and every other felon with admirers to shame. Entire websites dedicated to her would spread like wildfire. I can even imagine Penthouse or Hustler offering Allison money to take it all off. Since she would be in dire need of cash like her mother currently is, odds are she would accept the offer. I bet it would be their biggest selling issue ever.

The campus registrar recently sent me an email saying that all my classes for the upcoming semester have already filled up. I have also been offered the opportunity to write a book on Allison based on my experiences. I haven't accepted it, but it's nice to know people are interested. Maybe one day.

One night after some of the latest Dunbar family baggage was being aired on TV, Chloe asked me something I wasn't expecting.

"When people ask how we met and started dating, what are we gonna say?" I had thought of that myself and could never come up with an answer. But out of nowhere, I finally thought of something.

"We'll just tell them we met through a mutual friend."

GRANT BUTLER is an author from the Midwest who writes true crime and several genres of fiction. His literary influences include Stephen King, Ira Levin, Agatha Christie, and Thomas Harris. Cinema is also a big influence on his storytelling and some of his favorite films are Jaws, The Godfather, Goodfellas, and Psycho.

TWITTER @THEGRANTBUTLER